To [illegible]

with thanks

Sabine Hargreaves

16-09-10

Plane Crazy

Sabine Hargreaves

authorHOUSE®

AuthorHouse™ UK Ltd.
500 Avebury Boulevard
Central Milton Keynes, MK9 2BE
www.authorhouse.co.uk
Phone: 08001974150

First published by AuthorHouse 6/8/2010

ISBN: 978-1-4520-1850-8 (sc)

This book is printed on acid-free paper.

With special thanks to all my friends who supported me all the way, and to my enemies for making me stronger, and of course to Jet2.com who gave me the job of my dreams!

The episode with the postman

'Now – what on earth have I done with my keys?'

If only I had ten pounds for every time I have uttered this sentence, I could stop going to work, retire by the sea side and live a life of luxury. I could dine out for weeks, just on key stories. There was the time when I nearly got arrested breaking into my own house, add to that the incident where the keys ended up in an inconveniently placed manhole, and of course the unforgettable occasion where I had to climb onto my dustbin in a vain attempt to jump the garden wall wearing nothing but carpet slippers and pyjamas!

Like it or not, I have inherited the family 'anti key gene'! I am to keys what oil is to water. I am a disaster with keys! Just ask my neighbours.

A look of sheer relief spreads across my face as I locate the front door key just above my right ankle. Of course! The foolproof location, chosen carefully just after the incident with the belt loop and the garage door ... how could I forget!

I open the front door and dash into the hallway, immediately checking for mail – no luck as yet it seems. I can hardly wait for the mail this week! The slightest flap of the letter box sends me flying across the hall and breaking the land speed record!

I am in the kitchen now with a cup of tea, still thinking about keys, when I hear the familiar clonk of the mail on the doormat and off I dash knocking over my tea in the process. I tear open the front door and am face to face with Pete the postman.

I have known Pete for quite some time. He has delivered my mail for years and has been known to sit in my kitchen on the odd occasion, sipping a cup of tea and taking a break from the weather.

Recently though, he has seen a change in me. Far from being the calm and collected 'would you like to come in for a cup of tea' person, I have instead taken to ripping open the door and snatching the mail from him like a Rottweiler on speed. Today is no different and Pete is wearing his buy now familiar startled expression.

'Wait!' I shout, as I rummage through the pile of mail. 'There it is!' I shout even louder, triumphantly holding up a big white envelope. 'Don't go away!'

Pete's expression is changing from surprise to mild concern as he watches me dance around whilst I am trying to tear open the envelope. 'Yeah – we are celebrating' I exclaim enthusiastically as I grab Pete by the hand and drag him into the kitchen. 'Champagne – let's have champagne!'

I stop dancing and start wrestling with the fridge door producing a big bottle of champagne in the process. Pete is now wearing a stunned expression and I feel the time has come for an explanation before he has me sectioned.

'When something great happens in life you have to enjoy the moment. There is no point saying that you will celebrate when a friend can find a babysitter, or when the weather is better, or when you have lost two stone. There is only one way to celebrate and that is to do it NOW, right this very moment, and with gusto!'

So that's what we are doing. Well, that is what I am doing, with Pete still being a somewhat surprised and reluctant participant. A couple of glasses later though he is beginning to get into the spirit of things.

'I shouldn't really be drinking on duty you know, but as you say this such a special occasion, what the occasion by the way?'

I realise that I still haven't really enlightened him as to what this is all about, and I work hard to remain coherent as I finally launch into a comprehensive explanation.

' It's all about flying you see', I begin, it's been a dream of mine since I was six years old. I blame my father entirely, as it was him who decided to take the family to an open day at the airport, at the end of which I had to be surgically removed from the spectator gallery, apparently.

So naturally then , when I left school I applied to be a pilot, but when I left school female pilots did not exist, so that held me back a bit. I briefly toyed with the idea of becoming an air hostess, but that idea was soon dismissed by my father who said that no daughter of his was going to be a 'waitress', in the sky or otherwise, and that had been that! Had I been older, more mature maybe, I would have stood my ground, and I could have been one of the first female pilots that were recruited from the 'air hostess pool' and trained two years later. As things stood, however, I did as I was told, cut my losses, and trained in banking instead.

Shortly after that I decided to take the plunge, make use of my bilingual upbringing and move to England. I felt I would be better off in another country, far away from my father's overpowering influence. It was a quest for freedom, and the right to make my own decisions, so I could follow my dream to fly in peace and quiet.'

Pete is listening intently, whilst draining his glass yet again, and nods at me encouraging me to continue.

'I moved to Bournemouth, with a job in a local bank and the cock eyed optimism to believe that this was temporary. I found reasonable lodgings which I managed to turn into a small but comfortable home, and two part-time jobs in order to save some pennies.

Bournemouth had not been an accidental choice. It had a beach of course which is never a bad thing, but it also had something far more important: an airport, just the right size of airport at that. It was large enough to accommodate commercial aviation, yet small enough to still house a flying club including the obligatory club house with bar. It was at this flying club that I first took to the air, and I literally never looked back.

It all began with a trial lesson, a mini flight, just to see how I'd get on. It was all I expected it to be and more! We went up, climbed to about 2000 feet, went over Poole harbour, did lots of turns, laughed at traffic jams and came back in again. I was about to protest that I had not had my full 20 minutes in the air, when I realised I had in fact been airborne for over half an hour – time does indeed fly when you are having fun!

In the weeks leading up to my first flight, I.had learned a valuable lesson several times over: the weather can not only spoil your day, it can stop you from flying altogether. Despite of this slight but obvious drawback, I decided to go for it and signed up for my Private Pilots Licence training.

More part time work was required in order to get flying money. So I gave up my cleaning job in favour of Mac Donald's, which paid much better but had its own interesting moments.

I will never forget one fateful Saturday, fairly early on in my involuntary catering career, when I was busy making cheese burgers, and the boss turned around and instructed me to 'hold the onions'. This didn't make much sense to me at the time, so I put it down to the English sense of humour.

Must be some sort of in joke 'hold the onions, ha-ha'. I mean, who in their right mind would want to be seen standing in the middle of Mac Donald's, on a busy Saturday, in front of hungry crowds, holding a pair of onions! I wasn't going to fall for that one! 'I'm not telling you again,' my boss shouted, this time red in the face for emphasis, 'hold the bloody onions or we are going to have a riot on our hands'.

Oh well, if it makes the man happy, far be it from me to argue ...

It was only in the brief but fierce melee that followed that I got to understand the true meaning of the phrase. I realised at that point that I was a million miles away from being just 'one of the locals', but hey – all part of the learning experience!

Meanwhile on the home front the flying lessons took their slow and steady course, despite the winter weather, and in February my instructor had enough and jumped out.
'You think I'm flying with you again – you must be joking. Off you go and fly me a circuit'

And so I flew my first solo, which was the most frightening and at the same time most exhilarating moment of my entire life. Finally I was up there on my own, nobody shouting at me, nobody telling me what to do. There was just me, left to my own devices and relying on my hitherto accumulated flying skills, such as they were. Well, they were sufficient to fly a circuit and bring the aeroplane back in one piece, followed by a visit to the bar to get absolutely rat-arsed! I had gone solo – I was a pilot!!

Shortly after that I learned to navigate away from the field only to find it again an hour or so later, most of the time anyway. I learned about emergencies and how to deal with them and how to land at another airfield. We were plodding our way through the syllabus, and a few months later I gained my licence. I was 22.

What followed was one of the best summers of my life. I enjoyed my new found freedom and flew all over the place, taking up brave volunteers to help with the cost. Most of them enjoyed the experience, some of them were so keen to go again, they would give me their details so that I could call them whenever I had a spare seat. Word got around and before I knew it, I had a little black book of cost sharing passengers. I needed more seats, and so I found myself back at the Flying School, getting checked out on a four seater aircraft. The weather was playing game that year and I found myself airborne two or three times a week, carrying two or three passengers at a time, contributing towards my costs.

Flights more or less took the same pattern: We took off, behaved ourselves until we got to Wimborne, then we more or less did what we liked. I tried to accommodate my passengers' requests and most of them were standard stuff.

A lot of them enjoyed flying along the coast, some of them wanted to fly over their respective houses, others wanted me to take them somewhere. I didn't really care where I was going as long as I could build some flying hours and gain some experience.

There was one particular request that will always be with me, for a number of reasons. First of all I wasn't supposed to have done it. Secondly, when I did do it I managed to get it quite spectacularly wrong.

There was this old chap, who used to regularly visit the flying club. He came to all the 'Old Dam Busters' get-togethers and always had a story to tell, quite an interesting character by the name of John, who was always accompanied by his faithful old Labrador, Lancaster. The name I'm sure, led back to John's antics in the war but I never really found out. Anyway, the two of them were inseparable until one day, inevitably, Lancaster died.

John and I had struck up this unlikely friendship, based entirely on aviation, and as he approached me, in his grief, and asked me if I would be kind enough to take him up over the sea, so he could scatter Lancaster's ashes, I agreed.

Well aware that objects should not be dropped from aeroplanes, I was hesitant at first, but eventually decided to do the old boy a favour. So, off we went, out over the sea well past Hengistbury Head, where, having ensured no boats below could be engulfed in a mysterious ash cloud, I slowed down the aeroplane as much as I dared, so John could do the deed.

He opened the window and scattered .... and ... whoosh! A few seconds later the entire cockpit, was covered with what was left of Lancaster! We coughed and spluttered and I suddenly had to suppress fits of giggles, completely out of place for the occasion. Even John saw the funny side.

'Lancaster always liked a surprise,' he said. 'Let's fly home and find the Hoover'.

My little trips continued and the summer literally flew by and so did the next, and with winter approaching yet again it was time to hit the books and train commercially.

The books were not the problem, the course cost was! I'd spent the last two years applying for sponsorship, but all to no avail. The bank manager, in the days before the career development loan was invented, laughed and sent me home, and home could not help either. No amount of tin stacking, burger making and cleaning was going to get me anywhere near the amount of money required to take my commercial exams. I only had one option, and that was to save up and wait. However, whilst I was waiting, I was jolly well going to work in aviation.

A year later I found myself in a college of knowledge, at Bournemouth airport, working with student air traffic controllers. Using my radio skills to play the role of the aeroplanes and pressing buttons to make the targets move on the radar screen. It was interesting for the first few weeks and thereafter, to break the monotony of the job, we were allowed to do anything we liked as long as we kept working to a good standard. Some girls were painting their nails, or playing cards, or even reading magazines. I decided to dedicate myself to flying studies and got in a good two to three hours a day. When I found out that flying and air traffic exams were very similar, I asked to sit the theory exams for air traffic control, and to my own surprise – I passed them.

And so my life took an unexpected, although not entirely disastrous turn. I had turned from a flying wannabe into an air traffic control student. I figured that if I could not afford to become a pilot, then I would become an air traffic controller instead, earn plenty of money and fly for fun, at least for now. 'For now' would last many years and I became an air traffic controller at Southampton, then Gatwick and finally Stansted. It was a job I thoroughly enjoyed and as the months turned into years, I realised I was having a good time and a good standard of living.

My desire to fly had not gone away but was repeatedly put on the back burner. A change in exam rules put me off my first attempt, and then 9/11 brought the industry to a standstill. Suddenly I was in my mid thirties and I realised it was now or never. The tables had turned and I could afford it.

18 months of a 16hour days followed, as I was mixing work with commercial pilot studies. Holidays became ground school weeks and days off turned into exam days, and that, Pete, is what this letter is all about. This is the reason I have been running the door down at the sound of the letter box. These are my results!

This letter means that the exams are done and dusted, and that I can look forward to the expensive but far more entertaining flying part, and this is how I come to sit in my kitchen today drinking champagne.'

As I finish Pete is onto his fourth glass and entirely the worse for wear.

'This is quite a story,' he agrees as he makes several attempts to get up from his chair and fails.

Oh my God! I can just see it. The postman is going to be here for days, stuck in my kitchen, unable to move and in no state to leave… I will never live this one down!

Several attempts later Pete manages to get up and make it to the door.

'Hey, don't forget these,' I say as I pick up his mail bag.

God knows what is going to happen to all these letters. I must remember to deny all knowledge!

As Pete staggers off into the distance, I close the door and look at my letter again. I can't stop smiling! I'm now only a hundred lessons away from getting the job of my dreams.

The episode where timing is everything

I cannot help being excited as I am driving to the little grass airfield up the road, that would become the venue of many good and many bad days over the next few months.

If I could have managed to win the lottery in the last few years, I would probably be at Oxford now, enjoying full time training at one of the country's best flying schools, at an all weather airfield with super brand new perfectly equipped aeroplanes.

As it happens I did not win the lottery (and that is entirely my fault for not buying a ticket, which reduced my chances considerably) So I shall have to keep going to work like everybody else, and instead do my training when I can, and under very different conditions indeed.

I look on dismally as rain drops are exploding on my windscreen like fireworks. This does not bode well for my first day of training. Still – I must turn up and show willing.

As I approach Adam's Field, as it has been known since its world war II days, the clouds are on the deck and I can hardly make out the club house, the fleet of Cessna's and Arrows a sorry sight in the mist. Only the bar is busy.

There I bump into Jeremy and James, two of the flying club's characters. Jeremy used to be in the air force, long since retired, just likes to keep his hand in. He tends to come in on a Sunday, have a little flight, followed by a roast dinner in the club house.

James, by contrast, learned to fly in his mid seventies, in order to have days out and get away from his nagging wife (so he claims). She must be nagging him quite a bit, as James has always been highly motivated to improve and enhance his flying skills.

At first he got his private licence, then he learned to fly in bad weather, then at night. Eventually he spent his life's savings on a little aeroplane. Now he is off to France on a regular basis, enjoying a nice dinner and bringing back copious amounts of wine and cheese.

One day though, he got into trouble, and managed to stop all departures out of Heathrow. He was half way home across the channel, when he found an unwelcome stowaway, a wasp, which unfortunately he is allergic to. He desperately tried to get rid of the beast, which took much more time then he had anticipated. So absorbed was he in his task that he lost all sense of time and space and when he had finally got rid of the intruder, he found himself over a very large town in the south of England and deeply in the brown stuff. Thankfully he got away with a caution and has been paranoid about checking for wasps before every departure, even in the midst of winter.

Jeremy is a far more optimistic character, too optimistic sometimes, as he found out when he decided to fly to Norfolk for fish and chips, and ended up staying for three days as the weather changed suddenly.

'Never let a bad weather forecast get in the way of a good meal', he was alleged to have said as he had left Adam's Field earlier that day. Blessed with eternal optimism, he had to eat his words as well as his fish and chips, and has never really lived it down.

'Cup of tea?' Jeremy offers. I accept happily. 'Nice weather for ducks' he grins. 'That's because ducks can't fly' I retort, 'and by the looks of it neither can I, not today anyway'.

We sip our teas and observe the dismal scene outside. What a contrast to the many happy summers we have experienced here! Days with blue skies, light winds (ok – more often than not strong winds but who cared) and when you could see for miles! Days when we would go off to Clacton aerodrome, for a swim and a picnic, or up to Beccles for a visit to the local pub, for lunch and home made lemonade… not today!

'Who in their right mind starts a commercial course in November?' In comes Celia, who has previously been hiding in her office, buried in copious amounts of paperwork. She only has time for paperwork when the weather is bad. One whiff of a ray of sunshine and she is airborne as there is nothing else she would rather do.

With 20 000 hours on light aircraft (and nothing but light aircraft) Celia is well known in the industry. She is not only an expert, she knows how to bring out the expert in others. As the chief instructor and part owner of the flying club, she loves what she does and it shows. There is nothing Celia has not seen or cannot teach. I know I'm in good hands.

Celia's partner, Mark, is an events organiser and owns the other half of the club. He enjoys organising the social side as much as Celia enjoys the flying. Together they are a great team who create a good mix of flying school and social atmosphere.

Celia is inviting me into the classroom and gives me a copy of the commercial training syllabus.

'Basically it's nothing you have not seen before', she says,' it's just flying everything to a much more accurate standard'.

That sounds reassuring – or it would do if I could indeed remember what the private licence syllabus entailed. It has been so many years, and like someone who has had their driving licence for many years, I am bound to have developed some bad habits. We shall see.

Three days later the weather is looking much more hopeful, and Celia and I are in the briefing room getting ready for my first commercial training flight. I feel a touch nervous bearing in mind the huge expense at stake, but much more than that I am rather excited about the whole thing.

We get airborne and Celia is testing my navigation skills, which gives me a chance to get familiar with the Arrow, the most complicated aircraft I have flown up to this point. Not that the Arrow is particularly complicated really – but just now it is presenting a challenge.

The flight is progressing well and I am actually enjoying myself. I still seem to find my way from A to B without too much trouble and seem to be on top of the exercise.

Not all was to be smooth running though. My general handling skills leave a lot to be desired and Celia comes up with a plan: I am to have a few days of special training with an instructor from a different school, whom Celia describes as 'a little gruff, with bark worse than bite', but who apparently gets great results.

I know I do not respond well to the gruff and barking type and am approaching my three days 'special training' with some apprehension. However, this is not the time to show my sensitive side, and I decide to get over myself and get on with it.

My apprehension would turn out to be well placed.

As I walk into the bar for the first of my 'special sessions' a few days later, I realise that I must be early as I cannot see Dick Foster anywhere. Not that I know what he looks like exactly, but the only person I can see is an old chap drinking tea in the corner, who I assume must be the new ground man. Wellies covered in mud, jumper with lots of holes in it, white hair and beard yellowed by smoke. Surely this can't be...

I decide to be on the safe side and get on with my pre-flight tasks. Half an hour later, aeroplane at the ready and paperwork signed off, I am back in the club house, warming my hands on a cup of tea. Oh well, with a bit of luck he won't turn up.

'Bloody women, fannying around doing this and that, been here for half an hour and now you're sitting there drinking tea without a care in the world. Probably make me late for dinner. That'll be just my luck'.

Oh my God – it's him!

I'm sure he'll be very nice when I get to know him. I mean, I get on with most people, I'm famous for it. I probably have nothing to worry about! Probably get on really well with him in the end. Have a beer afterwards, laugh about my mistakes....

'Stand their goggling, another kitchen sink unattended to. You just get on with it. Start the donkey, I'll catch up with you when the bloody thing has warmed up. Shouldn't be out in these temperatures at my age. Bloody students!'

Then again...

With all preparations complete at last, we take off into the gloom. I am working hard and am getting good practice at developing a thicker skin at the same time. This alone was worth the extra lessons and would come in very handy in the months to come.

Plus, Dick is actually very good at what he does despite his gruff demeanour, and I seem to be picking things up reasonably quickly.

'Not like that! Bloody air traffic controllers, think they know it all'

(Why oh why did you have to tell him Celia?!).

'Probably do that again and like as not crash the bloody aeroplane and we'll end up in a field and I won't get to the pub. That'll be just my luck!'

I keep plodding on, motivated by fear rather than desire, telling myself that the sooner I get things right, the sooner this will be over. Huge relief then when, at the end of the week Dick announces me ready for test.

Organised as I am, I wisely took some leave at work. Two weeks in January, in order to do my commercial test, followed by two weeks in February to go skiing and recover. After two years of hard work I feel a holiday would be just the ticket.

Christmas passes in a blur. Although there is no flying for a week, I am still busy at my job at Stansted, but it feels like I am working part time. No studying and no flying, what on Earth am I going to do on my days off, not difficult I don't think!

As the New Year is starting and most people are getting back to work, I am looking forward to my fortnight off and to bringing my commercial course to its conclusion.

On Monday morning, Celia is coming in especially to put me through my paces. The skies look leaden and I hope the rain will hold off long enough to give us a chance.

As I get to the airfield, she has already arrived and is busy preparing the aeroplane.

'Good Christmas Celia?'

'Usual stuff' she says, 'too much food and too many screaming children'

I grin. Celia is not known for her tolerance of large amounts of noisy kids, but unfortunately is an aunt to five of them.

'Had to drink loads to drown them out' she continues, 'massive hangover on Boxing Day, threw up all over the turkey leftovers'.

I suppress a giggle. 'Oh, well, back to work to recover then', I console her. 'I promise not to scream'.

Whilst Celia continues with the aircraft preparation I get all the paperwork ready. The weather forecast does not look promising. Another two hours from now and we will be back to sitting in the clubhouse, talking about flying rather than actually doing it.

The Weather Rule of Thumb in aviation 'bad weather arrives early and good weather arrives late' seems to be applying today as always. Less than 30 minutes after getting airborne from the muddy field, we have to call it a day. Sheets of cloud are making it impossible to see, and the little Arrow is beginning to struggle in increasingly difficult conditions. We apply rule of thumb number two: 'better to be on the ground wishing you were up there, than up there wishing you were on the ground'. We head back to the field and put off the flying to another day. That's one day's leave down, thirteen to go.

I can hardly believe my eyes as an hour or so later, I am driving home in a blizzard. This cannot be happening! It *never* snows at Stansted. Well, it has been known to, but ever so rarely. It's bound to be one of those 10 minute flurries, and just as the kids get excited about getting the sledges out, it stops, never to be seen again for another five years or so.

But it keeps snowing, and snowing and snowing. I draw the curtains in frustration. I am meant to be back at the airfield at nine o'clock in the morning for another practice run, in order to attempt my test in week two of my leave, working on the basis that the weather will be flyable on one day out of seven in week two ... we will see.

As I open my curtains again the next morning I am greeted by a winter wonderland. My garden is covered by three feet of snow. The skies are a clear blue and it's perfect flying weather. All I have to do is to somehow get to the airfield. I can drive in snow. I mean I grew up in Germany where we had snow all the time! Driving in snow is practically part of the driving test over there. The roads will be clear – it will be no problem.

As I switch on the TV I rapidly change my mind. The Stansted Motorway is headline news and even Stansted itself is closed.

'... and we are asking motorists not to drive unless it is absolutely necessary'

I will have to admit defeat – at least for today. I do have a fortnight after all, or rather twelve days left now in which to do this - plenty of time, relax, it'll be grand.

The next day is a similar picture. However, the roads are being gritted and the area is slowly recovering from the deep freeze, but just for today the general advise on the news is to stay away from the roads if at all possible.

Eleven days to go and I will be back at work, and I have not flown for a fortnight! Then my luck seems to be turning:

Day three dawns bright and sunny yet again and it is finally safe to venture out onto the roads. I ring Celia to make sure I won't have a wasted journey.

'It's not impossible to fly off snow' she claims, 'I have done it before but we will first have to flatten it with the tractor.

The ground is frozen – so it should work. Come on over if you fancy a bit of an adventure.'

I do not need to be told twice. A quick bowl of porridge and I'm outside in my wellies, shovelling sand onto my drive, which is steep and at an odd angle to the road, which could make for an interesting combination, but needs must… Job done, I'm off to Adam's Field.

As I approach I see the tractor has already commenced its work, creating a narrow strip that could pass for a runway. The process is going to take some time yet and I get to work preparing the aeroplane and by now familiar paperwork.

Two hours later Celia and I are off into the still blue skies, and I am glad that I am in the air again.

It's a fantastic morning, the Essex countryside barely recognisable under all the snow. Celia puts me through my paces. I am enjoying myself, but my performance is disappointing. After all that preamble, I seem to not be as sharp as I was two weeks ago, and am told that more training is required if I wanted to pass my test first time.

'It's not just passing that's important. It's showing that you can pass something first attempt. Otherwise you are classified as a 'training risk' and will therefore have problems getting an interview, never mind a job', Celia explains. 'You are in the official 'training risk category' already, she continues, 'simply due to your age, unfair as it may seem, and therefore a first time pass is all the more important.'

There is no point arguing. I book some more training to get back up to speed. At least the weather is supposed to get warmer and after all I have over a week before I have to get back to work. So lets not panic!

The next day the weather is warmer. It's also considerably wetter. And so is the next day and the day after that. Everyday it's the same picture: a grey veil of cloud touching the ground, and fog melting into drizzle. In three days time my leave will be over and I'm going to have to go back to work. There is no way I'm going to do anymore flying this week, let alone my test! It's a mugs game!

To add insult to injury, my first day back at work dawns clear and frosty. In fact the entire week is perfect. Murphy's Law I suppose. I must work, come home and sit down to make another plan – fast!

There is no way I'm giving up my skiing holiday! A girl needs a break some time! So I am going to have my skiing holiday...

Half an hour later I am on the phone. My friends are very understanding.

'You wouldn't actually enjoy yourself' says Mike, 'you will be sitting on the slopes, miserable, asking about the weather in England and wishing you were there getting on with it – and then you'd ski off in frustration and break a leg or something'

'That's right', Sharon agrees, 'you'd be worrying about how to get more time off work to finish your course and about what it would be like to be known as the girl who nearly made it in flying, but then gave it all up to go skiing instead'

I do allow myself to chuckle at their rather overdramatic prognosis, but they have a point. 'Shut up already! I'm staying here. I'm just glad you're not mad at me!'

By the end of February the weather has picked up a little and things are looking hopeful. Celia and I have been up a couple of times and I seem to have recovered my standards. 'Your test date is on Friday, Good Luck', Celia says casually as I leave the club.

Oh my god! I've got a test date – in two days time! I'm not sure whether to be happy or nervous! In the end I'm both. I can't wait for Friday! I go home and glue myself to the weather forecast and am pleased to see that it's looking quite hopeful.

On Friday morning it's raining stair rods. The rain is so heavy, it's obscuring the house next door. Floods are pouring down the steps in my garden as the rain barrel is struggling to cope.

'Obviously not, no', says Celia as I speak to her on the phone a few minutes later, 'all I can say is re-book. In fact, why don't I give you Juan's number, he is the examiner, you can call him yourself. Maybe you can use your charm and book up more than one day in advance? Oh, he's Spanish by the way – so no jokes on the phone – he won't get them.'

Ok, action is required. I am on a roll and decide to all Juan straightaway!

'Hello, Juan?'

'Que? Ah... la senorita with the test, si, esta lloviendo ,no?'

'Yes, it is raining indeed and I was wondering whether you would be kind enough to do my test tomorrow, or could we possibly...'

'Manana, claro, nine a clock, see you there'

Click – the phone goes dead.

It is very kind of Juan to take my test on a Saturday. Maybe it would have been rude to ask him to book me in on all the following days as well. I mean – we only need one day – one ruddy day where it all comes together!

However, on Saturday I have no luck either.

'Yes Juan, esta lloviendo again, but thank you for considering me on a Saturday anyway, and ...'

'Sunday? Si. Weather better tomorrow. I go to church and then I come. Ten o' clock – see you there.' Click -

I do not believe it! I must have done something bad in a previous life or something! I was about to leave for the airfield just now, suitably nervous and clad uncharacteristically smart in my shirt and tie, when Celia rang to tell me that the Arrow's battery had flooded in the downpours and nothing could be done until Monday, when the engineers were back on site. There is no other aeroplane we could use and therefore she was sorry but the flight cannot happen until next week... arrrgghhhh!

I want it to rain today! None of this sunny stuff please – I want downpours! I want the skies to open, so I can look up from my book and say 'ha! a blessing in disguise, good job I didn't fly today but no! The weather is mocking me – it's a crisp clear winter's day and I will just have to live with it!

I will be going back to work on Thursday and here I am twiddling my thumbs – this is not good for my blood pressure!

'Juan? Lo siento! No flying today ... no ... the aeroplane ... it will be sorted tomorrow, so maybe Tuesday? The forecast is good and ...'

'Tuesday no! Is not possible! Is not possible Tuesday and Wednesday too! My mother – she have new windows and I go help! Is important. Is family business'

Ok – that's that! On Thursday I go back to work and I shall be kicking the furniture! Maybe I should have gone skiing after all!

Luckily Celia has a back up plan. 'I know this examiner down at Gatwick', she tells me later that day on the phone, 'who would be willing to do your test. She will come up on

Tuesday provided the weather is good, so be here for ten o'clock'.

There is hope, remote hope – but even so!

The episode with the unexpected turn

At nine o'clock on Tuesday morning the telephone rings.

'Why aren't you here walking up and down and looking panic-stricken?' Celia wants to know.

'I'm on my way just now', I reassure her.

I had to wait for Gillian Devreaux, my examiner for the day, to give me the go-ahead by telephone first. Her drive is longer than mine.

The weather does indeed look good, and Gillian is on her way up from Gatwick. This is my one chance today, my one and only chance to get this done before I go back to work. No pressure then, no need to be nervous really...

I go into 'get organised' mode. It's my secret weapon against the jitters.

When I get to Adam's Field, I have to scrape the ice of the aeroplane, and then the mud. I take care of the refuelling and finally dedicate myself to a mountain of paperwork which I prepare to an almost artistic standard. First impressions are everything!

I feel ready for the task ahead, but there is still no sign of Gillian Devreaux.

Celia is popping in and out of the clubhouse, sharing her day between myself and a bunch of students who are all wanting to get airborne now the weather has improved.

She beckons me over. 'Any sign of this 747 captain?' she wants to know.

Who? Gillian Devreaux? A 747 captain? Ohmygod! I didn't know that! Why does she have to be something high up like a 747 captain? And then there is muggings here, in her Arrow...I feel totally intimidated!

Thankfully it turns out that I couldn't have been more wrong! When my examiner finally does turn up, all apologetic, having been held up in traffic on the notorious M25, car keys in one hand, wellies in the other, I realise that I am dealing with a human being here.

'Gillian Devreaux' she introduces herself, 'pleased to meet you, lets just pop into the office and get the paperwork out of the way, and then we're off'. She grins at me 'Don't look so worried – we don't come here to fail people'.

In the little office at the back of the clubhouse Gillian is scanning my licences and then briefs me for the test.

'Ok, you have 45 minutes to plan your navigation trip and I would like you to find Benwick, a tiny grass strip just North of Cambridge'. She points it out to me on the map. 'After that we go off and do some general handling and emergencies, then we come back here and do the circuits, and that should be it.'

That sounds straight forward enough, except I have never been to Benwick before. Bearing in mind, that I have seen just about every little airstrip in the area during my training, and even went on an airborne photographic trip to remind myself what they all look like, this is a bit unfortunate. I will just have to be careful, that's all. If I find the wrong airstrip, I'll have had it!

Half an hour later we are on our way. I take off from the Easterly runway at Adam's Field, and at 500 feet make a left turn for Benwick. I point the aeroplane in a sensible direction and give my estimated time of arrival. I am now committed. More than three minutes either side of that time and I will fail that part of my test.

Thank you Mr Foster for shouting at me all those weeks, as it motivated me to come up with good estimates on a regular basis.

Half way to Benwick things are looking good. I seem to be on time and on track. There is a God!

On my estimate I must be over my 'destination', but how can I be sure?! Underneath me are lots of fields, all of which look much the same. I must be close – but I must be careful. Identify the wrong field and I will have had a very expensive day out, that's all.

I'm still not sure and decide to circle. That's allowed – just once! At last, there, underneath me appears to be a rather straight field which could pass for a grass runway and over in the corner are, what looks like – a couple of aeroplanes! I pretty sight at any time, but today, particularly delightful!

'I am at Benwick' I announce with glee.

'Divert me to Eye', comes the reply from my examiner.

Eye is good – I can do Eye. I went to Eye several times and I got it wrong a lot, frequently mistaking the little airfield next to it for Eye. So thanks again, Dick, for hitting me over the head with a clipboard – twice! I shall not get it wrong today...

First of all though, there is a military flying area to cross. Normally this does not pose a problem, just a routine radio call and then do as you're told. This time, however, the military area is manned by *Americans*. There have never been two nations so divided by a common language! This could be interesting.

Whenever you speak to Americans in the air, their response will start with 'understand' when clearly they do not!

'Understand – you want to, ah..., cross the area?' comes the predictable reply to my request.

'Affirm'

'Roger' replies the American controller

Roger is plane speak for 'understand' yet again, but means very little else. A 'roger' does not allow you to do anything, and it does not deny you to do anything either. It simply means 'I understand', and as such leaves you dangling, literally.

I wait – nothing! I am now approaching the boundary and really have to coax some sort of decision out of these people. So I repeat my request.

'Roger'

Something more pro-active is required here. 'Am I cleared to enter the zone?' I ask in desperation.

Please, please say yes! Otherwise I will have to fly around it, and that means recalculating my arrival time for Eye, and that is very difficult if one is flying in semicircles, and maths and aeroplanes don't mix! I swallow to suppress the feeling of panic rising up inside me.

'Kilo-Lima is cleared to enter the zone, maintain your heading and level, military traffic above and below you'.

I breathe an audible sigh of relief.

As I am crossing the zone I watch in awe as fast military jets whiz past me above and below, and I must admit it is more my sense of self preservation rather then my desire to pass my test at this point, that makes me maintain my altitude – to the foot!

The spectacle lasts for fifteen minutes, after which we pop out of the zone the other side, apparently unscathed. I allow myself to relax a little.

My mood lifts even further as in the distance, the unmistakable chimneys of Eye come into view. Luck seems to be on my side as I am well within my estimate.

'I am overhead Eye', I announce, this time far more confidently.

'Pretend it's foggy', says Gillian as she produces plastic screens which promptly obstruct my view.

I can no longer look out of the window and have to fly the aeroplane solely by reference to the instruments inside. We fly a few manoeuvres, then she announces 'I have control'.

This is my clue to literally let go, so Gillian gets to fly the aeroplane. As I let go, Gillian puts the aeroplane into a screaming dive.

'Recover!' she instructs.

I did not need to be told twice.

'I have control'. This time she is turning so steeply, I catch a glimpse of the fields around Eye in the side window. 'And recover!'

Again I take control and put the aircraft back into normal flight.

Slowly we work our way through stalls, engine failures and pretend fires. Finally Gillian seems to have seen enough.

'Tell me where you are!' she demands, as I look at my instrument needles and the map and determine a point.

'Okay then', she concludes, 'fly me back to Adam's Field!'

I cannot help feeling increasingly optimistic. Just the circuits now and I will be done, and I have never had a problem with those… until today!

Round and round the airfield we go as I demonstrate various take off's and landings. It's not essentially difficult, but it is work intensive and requires a lot of concentration. After almost two hours in the air my concentration levels are falling.

'Okay, last one', Gillian announces, 'glide approach to land.'

The idea here is to idle the engine when you think you can glide into the field. Cut the engine too early and you will not reach the field. Cut the engine too late and a lot of manoeuvring is required so as not to overshoot the field. Whereas the latter case is preferable, the ideal case scenario involves cutting the engine just at the right point. That point can only be judged visually, taking into account the wind.

Today the windsock does not show any movement. Officially the wind is calm, but in reality it will blow a bit from the right and a bit from the left, making judgement difficult. However, Celia has always taught me that, in case of doubt, I should cut the engine over the farm with the grey roof, so I'm sure that will work today.

I pull back the thrust lever and start my glide. It's looking good.

'What the ###?!'

I catch a brief but terrifying glance of a little Cessna coming from the wrong direction and cutting me up just before I reach the airfield. I have no choice! In goes the power and off we go for another circuit. I cannot believe it! I was seconds away from a safe landing and hopefully a passed test – and now I have to fly that manoeuvre all over again! I try not to show my frustration, but on the second go I'm feeling jittery. My air of serenity is gone and I am totally losing my nerve. I am actually shaking as I am preparing for the glide. I can't even see the farm with the grey roof. Christ – what am I doing! As I cut the engine I can see already that this is not going to work. I am nowhere near where I was last time. I decide to opt for safety and throw it away for another go, all the while feeling worse and worse.

Gillian takes control.

'Now look, you were unlucky there, that's all. Now let me just fly this thing around the corner and then I am giving you one last go. Now stay calm and do what you have been doing all day. I am more than happy so far.'

As I take control I am anything but calm but I know that I can do it. I take a deep breath as I set myself up for one last approach. I will give it everything. Even the farm with the grey roof has re-appeared. I cut the engine and start the glide. I seem a little high at first, so I put the gear down early to get some drag and then, as if there was nothing to it, I land right in the middle of the airfield.

We make our way back to the little office again, where I finally hear those words that I have been working towards for weeks:

'Congratulations, you've passed'.

Dick Foster is sitting at the bar.

'She passed, did she? That's another kitchen unattended to. Give the wife ideas. Probably have to go home and make my own tea. That'd be just my luck!'

The episode where I have to be inventive

The next morning I wake up in confusion - I am not entirely sure where I am. Is that … a toilet seat?

Now it all comes back to me. I felt sick during the night. That's it. I can distinctly remember getting up and making my way to the bathroom. I don't think I was sick actually – I must have thought better of it and then promptly nodded off face down on the toilet seat.

Oh God! I cringe as I look in the mirror. I am a curious colour of greyish white, with the imprints of the toilet seat engraved in a nicely contrasting red, just above my eye-brows! Good job I'm not going to work today! There must have been drink involved, a lot of drink!

Of course - I was celebrating! I passed my commercial test yesterday! Yey! I'm lost in the moment as I let yesterday's feelings of success flush over me again …but how on earth did I get home? I can't remember a thing!

Serves me right for being such alight-weight drinker! I just never seem to get the chance. I am always about to be working, or flying, or we are meeting in a pub miles away and I'm relying on my car. I am a "one drink on a good day" sort of person and you know what, that's ok, that's a good thing generally. However, the slight drawback here is that when I do drink properly it tends to have disastrous consequences.

Last night I was drinking properly - a message on my answer phone provides a little clue:

Hi, it's Celia. Well-done again, and don't go near the Fox and Hounds again for a while, eh? Just keep a low profile...

Ok – damage limitation, what happened in the Fox and Hounds? I must ring Celia.

Apparently, so the story goes, Celia and Mark had to carry me out of the pub, where I had been refusing all food in favour of more liquid sustenance. The landlord had been quite happy with that, until I started doing the aircraft fire drill using the pub's fire extinguisher. At that point he got pissed off and threw me out.

Aha, I see. No Fox and Hounds for a while then. It's rather a shame really. I always quite enjoyed the food in there.

I spend the whole day smiling despite my hangover. I would love to share my good news with postman Pete, but have not seen much of him recently. To be honest I have not seen much of him since the summer, since the champagne session to be precise.

My neighbours inform me that he does not tend to hang about much anymore in Honeybourne Close. He quickly delivers his letters, then runs for the hills.

I suppose he did get into a bit of trouble after our little celebration, mixed up the odd delivery, putting the odd letter through the wrong letter box during the afternoon...

He probably would have got away with it, had he not delivered the Ann Summers Order to Bertha Stubbs at number 35. A mistake easily made, that caused Mel and Sonya at number 53 to have a fairly boring afternoon in, whilst the old bat at number 35 took it personally and put in a complaint. You can't keep some people happy!

With a jolt I realise that I will have to go to work myself in the morning, and get things right, especially tomorrow! I am still (and will be for some time) and air traffic controller and do not want anybody to think that I am losing interest in the job now that I am otherwise qualified, albeit only just.

The next morning I am quite pleased I am at work, as I will need to sit down in the break and plan my next step. I will need to see when I can book leave in order to do my instrument rating.

The instrument rating (IR as it's known) is the BIG ONE. It is a very precise exercise in instrument flying and money spending, thousands and thousands of pounds, the exact amount depending on how successful the project is. A first time pass is even more important here than in the previous test and no chances must be taken. Therefore I will not even consider doing this part time.

Organised as I am, I have been saving leave from the previous year and that, together with this years leave, will give me the ten weeks off required to complete my course. I have even found a training organisation. All I have to do is pop downstairs and book my leave with the boss.

'You want what?' I almost shout as I am in the boss's office ten minutes later. I cannot believe what I have just heard. I am gob-smacked! 'Why on Earth should I have to give a years notice to take my own leave?

'Taking the leave is not the problem. It's taking all that leave at the same time, which is making things difficult for staff planning,' argues Ian.

Reluctantly I admit that he has a point. From his point of view there is nothing to be gained by sending me away for ten weeks at a time, in order to obtain a qualification that will eventually take me away from my present job. I quickly realise that getting angry is not going to help me here. I try a different approach.

'Ok, this is very important to me. So what can I do to make this happen?'(Please don't tell me I have to resign. That would be somewhat premature and also deeply worrying. Please help me out here...)

'How about this,' he suggests. 'You give me ten months notice in writing, and we will confirm in writing that you will definitely have the leave. You realise also of course, that you will lose your licence currency here in the tower and will have to retake the exam on your return.'

Gulp! I didn't think of that! How could I not have realised that being away for more than 60 days would mean having to retake my Stansted exams!

'Of course, no problem, I can do that,' I say with a confident smile that betrays how I'm really feeling as I walk out of the office.

Oh crap, oh crap, oh crap! This is all a lot more complicated than I had anticipated! Not for the first time I am asking myself if I am opening a can of worms here. Do I really and truly want to put myself through all this? Do I want to fly that much, or am I just like a dog with a bone that won't let go of something for fear of losing face. It is not too late; I could just call it a day. I decide to definitely sleep on things before I make decisions that I might regret.

A couple of days later, and after some soul searching, I decide that I really do want to fly that much. I also feel that if I don't go for it, I will look back one day and regret that I did not follow my dream.

The exams I can handle. But ten months wait for my leave! What am I supposed to do for ten months?!

I am sitting in the staff room looking for the silver lining. Allegedly every cloud has got one and I know about clouds! So where is it?

Well, the obvious advantage is that I will have no problem getting a place on the IR course this far ahead. So let's get on with that one to start with.

A couple of hours later I am on the phone to Lucy, the secretary at 'Professional Flyers' in Bournemouth, the school I finally settled on as my chosen course venue after weeks of research. Lucy is pleased to hear from me, yet at the same time surprised to hear I won't be attending for another ten months.

Once I explain the situation though, she is quite sympathetic.

'You know, one day, you will be done with all this', she says, 'and you will look back at this from the cockpit of your airliner and laugh'.

I promise to bear those cheerful words in mind and book myself in for January 2005. I am keen to prepare myself in some way, but Lucy reassures me that all will be taught on the course, and the best thing to do is no preparation whatsoever.

However, she does advise me to book my accommodation well in advance and promises to send a list.

The promised list arrives two days later. It feels quite odd looking for a place to live in a town that was *home* for so long. A lot of the places sound familiar, and a lot of the familiar places appear to have doubled in price.

Compared to the rest of the course cost the accommodation issue is a mere bagatelle, but still – I cannot afford to go mad. On the other hand I need to live somewhere comfortable … Eventually I settle on a place on the seafront in Southbourne, a couple of miles from the airport.

Again, the landlord expresses surprise at my relatively early booking, but is happy with the arrangement provided I pay him a deposit.

The very next morning the deposit is on its way and I have secured a place at Sands Resorts. The whole venture may as yet be a long time away, but things are beginning to take shape. I am feeling a little better.

Still, I cannot afford to waste ten months – it seems such a waste! In those ten months I shall need to keep up my flying skills, ideally in the little Arrow. I need to fly at least once a week and that will cost me about … £5000! So, I'd have to spend another £5000 just to be exactly were I am now….

And then it hits me! I am going to make those flying hours count, I am going to do my flying instructors course. That will also cost me £5000, but I will gain another qualification.

And I can do the course part time – at Adam's Field, with Celia!

"Some people are glutton for punishment but by all means, come on over and we can discuss things", Celia is quite happy to have some company on another rainy afternoon at Adam's Field.

Her reasoning convinces me that I am making the right decision.

'The course involves both flying and ground school, but nothing too taxing,' she reassures me. 'There is nothing you haven't seen before; you will just have to learn the teaching aspect. The exam involves a presentation and a flight test, which I have not known anyone to fail as yet.'

I am warming to the idea by the minute. 'When can I start?' I am getting really keen now.

'The courses normally run full-time for a period of two weeks. However, bearing in mind your work scenario, I could slot you into the gaps here and there. We have ten months, so there is no hurry, is there?'

Indeed there isn't. Celia is giving me quite a relaxed picture here. It all looks like the ideal solution. My mind is made up. 'Where do I sign?'

That afternoon it's all been organised. With a touch of apprehension I had parted with yet another chunk of money, and signed on the dotted line.

I'm now officially on the course starting next Monday.

The episode with lots of mishaps

I am not entirely sure what to expect as I turn up for day one of my instructor course. Surprisingly it is not raining today which has got to be a promising start.

I enter the clubhouse and look around expectantly wondering if any of the unfamiliar faces there might in fact be my course colleagues. Celia interrupts my thoughts as she beckons me into the back office, which would be our classroom for the next few months.

There are three other people on the course. To my surprise all of them are Irish. It turns out that this particular instructor course is so famous in Ireland; there are queues of people waiting to get a place. I realise that Celia must have done me a huge favour accepting me at such short notice. I also realise that this must be a very good course indeed.

After a brief introduction Celia gets on with what would become 120 hours of ground school. It's not just reminding ourselves how we first learned to fly, it's being able to teach it in both theory and practice that matters now. I find myself struggle a little remembering all the ins and outs, and am hoping that things will come back to me in time.

The theory of day one over with, we take it in turns to get airborne with Celia, who is doing her very best to be the worst 'student' in the world.

As I am trying to 'teach' her to fly around the airport, she repeatedly asks me how she is doing, and it is my turn to remind her with great diplomacy that she should be concentrating on the task in hand, rather than asking me how she is doing. However, it isn't until we are heading back towards the runway that I really come unstuck.

'How am I doing?' Celia persists.

I fall into the trap. 'I think you are possibly a little high' I remark cautiously.

The very next second we are diving almost vertically at the fields below. 'AArrgghhh!'

'A good instructor never panics. Students will try and kill you all the time. Just do something about it,' Celia reverts back to instructor mode. 'We'll try that again some other time.'

For the following few sessions I decide to not be entirely unprepared for whatever Celia decides to throw at me. Of course nothing untoward happens. No doubt she is waiting for me to get firmly re-established in my comfort zone before she pulls her next stunt.

As the course progresses we slowly make our way through the entire private pilot's licence syllabus. Ground school days mix with flying days as we progress, the choice depending largely on the weather and my shift pattern at work.

Only my fellow students change. The course is, after all, a fortnight's full time venture, rather than a part-time exercise that stretches over months, so I constantly meet new students that have only just started one minute and seem to be finished the next, whilst I keep plodding along at my own steady pace, but that doesn't matter. There isn't any great pressure and I just carry on as best as I can, wherever I can fit in the gaps.

Weeks turn into months and on yet another Monday, half way through yet another course with a new group of people, it is finally my turn to progress to 'pairing up'. During this final part of the course, students have learned enough to go up with each other and try out their newly developed instructing skills. I am teamed up with Eamonn, who stems, not surprisingly, from Ireland.

Eamonn has managed to find a job with a regional airline, but is not due to start for another six months. He is no stranger to instructing having spent the last three years 'falling out of the skies over Dublin' as he cheerfully puts it, and this is his refresher course.

The little Cessna slips and slides along through the Adam's field mud, slowing down to a snails pace and occasionally threatening to get stuck altogether as Eamonn and I make our way to the end of the runway.

Adam's Field has always been suffering from muddy winters. (It is not even winter yet, it's November but you could easily be fooled into thinking otherwise.).

A couple of years ago the mud problem affected business to a point where action was required. Help arrived in the form of wire netting, placed just under the grass in order to give the runway surface more strength and mud-resistance. The venture was quite successful and the runway became usable in almost any conditions. However the area around it is still bog standard grass, with a special emphasis on 'bog'.

Since the re-construction, the general rule has always been 'if you can make it onto the runway it's safe to go'. So, making it across the mud and onto the runway has become the ambition of every winter flyer, and more often than not, the odd pilot has had to be rescued by the ever-present tractor, parked conveniently in the field around the corner.

I must admit that in the last few minutes we, too, almost became tractor bait. However, as it stands we are still moving, albeit at the expense of having covered everything else on site in a spluttering of mud. The delight on our faces as we finally make it on to the runway!

'Thankfully this is just one of those little airfields where you just look and go,' I remark with glee, 'rather than wait for some clearance from the tower.'

'Just as well', comments Eamonn, 'if things were different, nobody would ever get away. Once you stop, that's it. People would all be stuck in the mud at various points along the grass verge, some probably not found until years later, in feet deep and beautifully preserved.'

I am still giggling as we are rolling down the strip, 60 knots, and we're off!

Every time I get airborne, even today, I get this feeling of freedom and exhilaration. The world looks so small from up here and all its problems so tiny and insignificant. You literally feel on top of it, which I suppose in a way, you are.

Eamonn and I are making our way over to the Essex coast and soon start practising a few exercises. I am to be the 'student' for the first part, and I try and listen and do *exactly* as I'm told. I take all instructions literally, and soon find myself doing stupid things. Eamonn has too much experience to be fooled though and keeps putting the aeroplane back on the straight and narrow. No matter what I try and do, he won't let me get away with it.

After thirty minutes we swap roles and it's now his turn to be the 'student'. I try and give unambiguous step by step instructions and he seems to be following them ok, with the odd little trick thrown in, which I pick up and correct.

Some of these things would have thrown me a few weeks ago. I am genuinely pleased with my progress. Things are ticking along nicely, the hour is flying by, and soon it is time to return to the field.

'Excuse me, instructor, but I cannot land. There seems to be another aeroplane on the runway,' says Eamonn as we overfly the airfield in order to circle and land.

'Ah, don't worry,' I try and come up with a few reassuring words. 'By the time we have flown around the airport he will be gone. It will take us a couple of minutes to do that and he knows that.'

One should always share one's 'experience' with the students, and I am getting well into character here. Actually I think I'm doing rather well.

'Errr…he's still there,' Eamonn remarks a couple of minutes later.

Ok, now would be a good time for him to move. I mean, he can't be stuck or anything. He's on the runway. You never get stuck once you are on the runway. We'll be down in a couple of minutes. So this would be his window…

Eamonn snaps out of student mode. 'Can you hear him on the radio? Sounds like he is looking for some sort of take-off clearance. He keeps reporting ready and revving up his engine.'

I am sorely tempted…

'Go on, do your bit,' encourages Eamonn, 'it's not like the words won't roll of the tongue now'.

Well, I shouldn't of course, but it's either that or we'll be circling until this chap works it out, which will cost phenomenal amounts of money. What the hell! I press the radio button:

'Golf-Mike-Tango clear for take-off runway 27, the wind is variable five knots.'

Promptly the little aeroplane starts rolling down the runway.

'If my boss knew about this, it would be tea and biscuits in the office. I'm sure

I'm not supposed to do this sort of thing anywhere else but at Stansted'

'Ah, I won't tell him,' replies Eamonn, and this way it'll be a landing and tea and biscuits in the clubhouse instead.'

I must admit he has a point.

Eamonn is ready to revert back into student mode and grabs the controls, white knuckles and matching expression on his face. 'I don't think I can land', he claims, 'I have forgotten how to do it entirely.

I forget all diplomacy. 'Eamonn, you will land of this approach. If you go around after all that kerfuffle, I will jolly well shoot you and fly the bloody thing myself.'

At the end of the week, Celia takes me up to check on my progress. She dots a few i's and crosses a few t's and promptly pronounces me 'ready for test', to be taken in the middle of December.

'I am not going to be nervous this time! This is not an essential part of my flying career, just a little bonus that's all. I should just go and enjoy the day!'

I am talking to myself as I am trying to calm my nerves on the day of the test. I cannot believe that they are hordes of butterflies flying around in my stomach. It's me who should be doing the flying here.

I calm down a little as I reach Adam's Field. The weather is good for once, the examiner has arrived from Stansted and everything seems to go as planned this time.

Two hours later I'm done! I am a flying instructor, I can hardly believe it! What a superb Christmas present!

We are in the bar, Eamonn, myself and two others, celebrating our respective test results. It wasn't so bad in the end. We had to give a lecture and then go flying for an hour and a half to demonstrate our newly found teaching skills. Before I knew it, it was over and here we are, back in the club house in time for Happy Hour.

'Orange juice?' Celia is aghast. 'Look around you. All flying instructors, all pissed! You are going to have to learn to up your alcohol intake you know,' she adds, tongue in cheek.

'Well, I'd love to Celia,' I retort, 'but unfortunately I am going to have to go to work in a couple of hours. Night shift, you see. So strictly off the juice I'm afraid. Bloody shame really!'

Then again, this might be a good thing. I have not been back to the Fox and Hounds as yet!

Christmas is a happy one! I have had a good year and am full of anticipation for my course in January!

I have even had a chance to try out flying instructing. Celia has given me a couple of 'trial lessons', so that I am not entirely 'green' anymore.

The more experienced instructors do not seem to like the trial lessons, which involve members of the general public having a go at flying an aeroplane. I quite enjoyed taking up my two 'students', a father and a son who had the lessons as their respective birthday presents. They flew, one after the other, and had an equally good time over the Essex country side, flying for thirty minutes each and taking photos of their houses at the same time.

For me the highpoint of the day was actually getting paid for flying, for the first time ever! It may not have been much but the point is I went flying and actually got *paid* for it. That was quite a turn up for the books!

Before I know it the year has come to a close and I find myself in January. My New Year's resolution is to finish my commercial flight training without failing anything. I am counting down the days to the beginning of my course. I know it's going to be tough, I know it's going to have its moments, but to be frank I can hardly wait!

On January 9th I find myself driving down the M3, direction Bournemouth, singing along to the radio. I am not allowed to sing in public, as, what I lack in skill I make up for with enthusiasm, which does not give the result the public wants to hear! Good job I'm in the car and safely out of earshot.

My little MX5 is packed to the gunnels with everything I need, and a lot of things I don't need, and anything else in between, that would fit in and wasn't actually nailed down or attached to the house.

Three hours later I arrive in Bournemouth. The weather is glorious. As I approach the seafront, the winter sun is reflected in the water as Southbourne beach stretches out in front of me. I keep a lookout for Wave Crescent and finally pull up in front of Sands Resorts.

The place is not quite as grand as the name suggests, but I notice with relief that it looks clean and tidy. I walk around to the side entrance and ring the doorbell. The landlord appears on the door step and introduces himself.

'Hi there, I'm Karl'. I recognise his voice from the phone conversation a few months ago.

He shows me into the cosy kitchen. 'Will you be wanting an evening meal today?' he wants to know.

'Actually, that would be nice.' I am delighted with that prospect! My flying will involve a degree of shift work over the next few weeks and I decide to take every opportunity that presents itself to grab a decent meal, right from the start.

Karl picks up my suitcases (the rest of my stuff will have to be unpacked later) and takes it up to my room. The room in itself is lovely, but on the way up we dodge several buckets of paint, paint rollers and brushes.

'Ah, I must apologise for that,' he says, 'we are currently in a decorating phase, but it should be finished within the next fortnight.'

I tread carefully as I go back to the car to fetch the rest of my stuff. What on earth made me take so many things? A beach mat in January - I must have been mad!

Finally everything is put away and it's still two hours to dinner. I decide to take a stroll along the beach. The sun is still shining as I set off. Maybe this is a good omen for the weeks to come.

On Monday morning I am on my way to the airport to start my course with 'Professional Flyers'. I pick my way through the rush hour traffic. Bournemouth may have changed, but the traffic congestion is definitely as bad as before, if not worse.

Finally I drive through the airport's main entrance, past the terminal, where I soon spot the 'Professional Flyers' flag on the left. I find a space in the car park and get out. So this is it. I take a deep breath and make my way to reception.

My initial expression is one of total and utter chaos. There are books in every corner, the reception desk is covered in manuals, and to top it all the whole room smells distinctly of dog.

Seconds later I discover the reason why, as a Dalmatian gets up from a bed in the corner and starts sniffing the new arrival. I'm not all that good with dogs, but this one seems quite harmless.

'Ah, he knows you have sandwiches in your bag, a head rises behind the mountain of books and I am looking at Paula, the school secretary. 'Just you make sure you never leave your flight bag where he can get to it. He's been known to make his way in and gobble up everything inside, edible or not. Come on Baxter, on your bed.'

The dog obliges and I get the chance to introduce myself.

'We've been expecting you,' Paula smiles at me. 'You will be doing some theory today with your instructor. You've got Archie, he's great. He's Lucy's husband.'

On hearing her name, Lucy opens the door of her office. 'Oh, hello there, she greets me.' The voice sounds familiar, but she does not look at all like I imagined her. 'I see you've arrived. Welcome to the school! I leave you in Paula's capable hands.'

The door was open just wide enough for me to catch a glimpse of her office, which by all accounts had the same chaotic look about it as the reception desk. Despite that first impression however, things seem to run like clockwork in here. So I must not judge a book by its cover.

Paula gives me a guided tour of the school building. The kitchen (I remind myself to use it as little as possible), the students lounge, a few offices and four briefing rooms.

She opens the door to one of them. 'This is your room for the day,' she says. 'Just leave your stuff in here and get settled in, and remember, sandwiches out of reach. Archie is flying but should be with you shortly. Maybe you would like to fill in these forms in the mean time. Any questions, you know where I am.'

Left to my own devices in the little briefing room, I feel a mixture of apprehension and excitement. The room consists of a desk for two, a white board and an array of pens, small but functional. So this is it. I'm finally here, and this is going to be the 'big course'.

I busy myself filling in the registration forms and, having deposited my flight bag including my sandwiches safely on the high window sill, leave to hand in the paperwork at the front desk. I am just about to make my way to the coffee lounge, when the door opens and a tall man with a moustache enters the room. He has a professional air about him. This must be Archie...

Half an hour later Archie and I are in the class room and he is telling me about the course.

'We will be flying a Duchess which is fairly sedate and forgiving,' he begins, 'and an excellent tool for the job in hand. The first week we will attempt to pass the twin rating, which will enable you to fly legally on a two engine aeroplane, which is a requirement for this course. Week two to eight are then spent training for and eventually passing the famous IR test.'

I am taking all this in. I like Archie's professional and no-nonsense approach. We are going to get on just fine.

'How did you enjoy your commercial course?' Archie wants to know.

I give it some thought. 'Well, it had its moments,' I say eventually. 'It ranged from the mildly disorganised to the wildly surprising, largely due to the weather and associated circumstances,' I add cautiously, 'but it worked out all right in the end and I passed first time,' I add quickly and not without pride. I decide not to mention the fiasco with the circuits.

'Well, this course will take an organised and steady pace by comparison,' reassures Archie. 'The bad weather does not matter so much after week one, in fact we welcome bad weather as that is what you are training to fly in. However, we require hard work and dedication, if you want to pass first time and in the limited time available to us.'

Well, ideally I want to pass this course well ahead of time. No point sitting here, with one week to go before I have to re-appear at Stansted, and putting pressure on myself that I have to pass in that last week. So, hard work and dedication you have, my friend.

'Of course,' I say out loud. 'I have chosen to do this full-time, so I can work as hard as possible, and the dedication really comes with the territory.'

The introduction over with Archie proceeds to show me various instrument flight patterns, which I will eventually have to produce in the aeroplane with great accuracy. Before we know it lunch time is upon us, and I make my way to the student lounge, to meet my course companions.

The coffee lounge is busy and is clearly the social hub. I meet some of my fellow students, all different ages, all with different backgrounds and all at different stages of the course.

There is Rowan from Ireland who has a job lined up already, provided he gets through the course. There is Pete who is an ex-police helicopter pilot trying to make his way in fixed wing flying. The chap next to him introduces himself as Gary, and I recognise Adie as one of the guests in my hotel.

There is a lot of shoptalk going on. Today everyone is excited as Sandy is 'on test' having come to the end of her course. Sandy is the only other girl on the course at the moment and is hoping to join a regional airline if she passes today. I remember someone leaving as I came in. That must have been Sandy going across to the test centre. She must be feeling pretty nervous right now. I hope she passes!

Sandy does indeed pass, another credit to the school's high success rate.

I must admit I feel a touch envious as we sit in the pub that evening to celebrate, as is the school's tradition. Sandy has just aced the one thing that everyone else around this table is still working hard to achieve. It took her just over six weeks apparently. That sounds promising bearing in mind my fairly tight schedule.

Earlier this afternoon I had my first lesson in the aeroplane. The weather was not too bad and I must admit I enjoyed flying the Duchess and did not make too bad a start according to Archie.

They want me back first thing in the morning. So I best not have a late night, as much as I am enjoying myself. Rowan especially has had me in stitches the entire evening. There is something about the Irish sense of humour that sets me off every time.

The next day I am getting airborne twice in the Duchess. Archie is trying to get me ahead of the schedule as bad weather has been forecast for the end of the week. I am in luck though. I manage to fly on Wednesday and my twin rating test is booked for Thursday morning. It's just a quick hour and a half and I am told that I have passed. No drama and not too much excitement this time. Long may it continue!

The rain finally does set in on Friday as I make my way back home on the motorway, but that's fine by me. Just as well I did not fly today, as I had some serious accommodation issues to sort out.

As I arrived back at the hotel on Thursday night with a big grin on my face at having had a successful first week, Karl the landlord's expression immediately dampened my mood.

'Could I have a quick word before you leave this week?' he wanted to know.

I looked at him with a mixture of foreboding and undisguised curiosity.

'Well, the thing is', he continued, 'our redecorating plans have taken an unexpected turn, in that, for reasons only known to themselves, the painters will have to finish by next weekend.'

I looked at him, encouraging him to continue.

'... and unfortunately that means we will have to close the hotel for a week; that is until next Sunday.'

'So that means...,' I tried to second guess where this was heading.

'That means we have made alternative arrangements for you, to stay in the hotel opposite for a week.'

He looked at me hopefully as I nodded understandingly.

'... although that would be more expensive.' He had delivered his punch line.

'How much more expensive?' I wanted to know.

Quite a bit more expensive, it turned out. In fact, so much more expensive that I was forced to look elsewhere, if I was to avoid busting my budget at this early stage.

The first thing I did was to ask for my deposit to be returned, and therefore my freedom to make any decision I might consider reasonable. Karl did not hesitate, immediately realising that he was in no position to argue.

'I think about it over the weekend and let you know.' I said, keeping my

options open.

My next stop was the office of 'Professional Flyers' to have another look at their accommodation list, but as it turned out, I didn't even need to go that far.

In the office, crouched over Paula's desk, was Sandy, busy signing all the paperwork following her successful test.

'How are you?' Sandy greeted me with a big grin despite her hangover.

I explained my dilemma and Sandy's grin widened.

'You are in luck,' she said. 'Once I've finished this lot, I'll be on my way to my digs to pack my stuff and go back to Manchester. I'm pretty sure they'd love to have another tenant. Why don't you let me give them a quick call and you can probably follow me down there and see how you like the place.'

I was made up! From Sandy's description the house sounded lovely.

Half an hour later we were following each other down the little country road leading away from the airport, and to the country house that had been Sandy's temporary home. I was not to be disappointed.

The room was warm and cosy, the whole place squeaky clean, and if I stayed there until the end of my course, I would save lots of pennies. Alison and Jo were absolutely charming and only too happy for me to take over from Sandy. I had fallen on my feet!

My head is full of the events of the first week as I make my way up the motorway. The drive is slow in the by now steady Friday afternoon traffic and the weather is not helping. I decide to leave much later next time to avoid the rush hour.

Either way, I will not be home until about 9pm, so I might as well wait next time, until the roads stop resembling a car park.

My weekend at home is flying by. I spend the entire Saturday washing and ironing and then packing my stuff for week two. There is no food in the house, either, so I have to join into the Saturday morning supermarket frenzy whether I like it or not.

Saturday night is spent in the Fox and Hounds (at last!) to update my friends with my progress.

Sunday morning dawns before I know it, and there is still a lot of stuff to sort out and a car to pack. This time I'm going to be more sensible. The beach mat can stay at home.

I am actually quite excited about moving into my little room this evening. There is no food provided this time of course, and the shops will be closed when I get there. So another trip to the supermarket just before I leave, I think. Self catering will fit in well with the 'shift work' aspect, but I will need to be organised. Where is this day going?!

After dinner, I tackle the inevitable phone call to Karl at Sands Resorts. I am not expecting this to be easy and indeed I shall not be disappointed.

As I explain to him that not only will I not take him up on his alternative hotel option, but that I will not come back to his place at all, he is spitting feathers. I can't blame him really, but take comfort in the fact that it wasn't I who upset the arrangement in the first place, and once circumstances had to change I might as well make sure that they change in my favour. I cannot help feeling a touch guilty when I first put the phone down, nonetheless.

It's time to get in the car and drive back to Bournemouth.

The episode with the unexpected hurdle

Alison is expecting me and opens the front door as I pull onto the drive.

'Cup of tea?' She offers as she shows me into the kitchen.

'That would be heaven,' I accept gratefully, pleased that my three hour drive is behind me.

'So, you are the new Sandy then,' Jo joins us and Alison winks at me.

'Just ignore him,' she says. 'He is always taking the Mickey.'

We finish our teas. The two of them explain the house rules and I hand over the rent. The business part over with; they show me up to my room, which immediately feels like home. I busy myself unpacking my car, and getting myself settled in. It doesn't take long this time.

On Monday morning I make my way up the perimeter road to the airport. There is far less traffic here than in Southbourne, and I am grateful the journey is much shorter.

At 'Professional Flyers' the day has already started.

'Good morning Paula, good morning Baxter,' I shout cheerfully as I make my way past the office.

'Briefing room two please,' replies Paula, currently with my back to me as she is scanning the activity board. 'Archie will be in any second.'

This is beginning to feel familiar. It's like I have been here for weeks.

'Welcome to the IR course' are the opening words of Archie's lecture. He begins to draw flight patterns and procedures on the board and gives me tips on how to fly them. It all looks incredibly complicated as far as I am concerned. I will have a job drawing them, never mind actually flying them.

'The best thing to do is to practice with a pencil on a piece of paper first,' Archie seems to pick up on my sense of awe, 'then, once you can remember the sequence, we have a go at flying them in the simulator.'

Well, I'd better remember them sooner rather than later – even at this early stage I am aware that I am on a limited time scale here.

I spend the rest of the morning tracing holding patterns with a pencil. By midday my pencil is worn out and I decide to have a walk to the airport terminal to buy another one, and a sandwich whilst I'm there.

I am amazed how much the terminal has changed, not necessarily for the better. What used to be a huge cafeteria has since moved airside, leaving very little room for a mini café and a newsagent. I opt for a take-away sandwich and make my way back to the school's common room, which, surprisingly, is deserted. They must all be out flying somewhere. I eat my lunch in silence and retreat back to my classroom in order to continue my exercises, new pencil at the ready. These patterns are beginning to feel second nature.

Not one minute too soon!

'Three o'clock in the simulator,' announces Archie as he re-appears after taking Baxter for his lunch time walk. That should be fun. I will finally get to fly my pencil patterns.

At first I am disappointed. I am not entirely sure what I imagined I would find, but the simulator looks just like a box from the outside. Somehow I had expected something a bit more plane-like.

Once inside though, I rapidly change my mind. By all accounts, I might as well be sitting in an aeroplane. I can even look outside onto what seems to be the runway at Bournemouth.

'It all feels so real,' I remark with enthusiasm.

'That's the general idea,' says Archie. 'We want you to treat it as 'real' as well. This is not a game.'

I should think not, at silly £ an hour I think to myself, as I am waiting to be told what to do.

Archie is behind me, in what looks like a little office, and uses a computer to set up the simulator. Suddenly I find myself, engines running, at the end of the runway for take off.

'Clear for take-off,' announces Archie, and I do my thing.

As I get airborne, the movements of the box are so true to life that I can hardly believe I am in a simulator. I am now in cloud and the 'aeroplane' flies along nicely, occasionally giving in to a bit of turbulence. I have completely forgotten that I am not in the air.

Archie, meanwhile, acts as both my instructor and air traffic control, and I listen carefully to what I am supposed to do next. It's amazing how much the financial aspect of things sharpens one's senses. I have never listened so well in my entire life.

We end up practising the holding patterns, which I had been drawing all morning, and I am amazed how well I can remember everything I have to do. The pencil method is obviously working.

I am actually enjoying myself, despite the pressure, and before I know it the hour is up, and I find myself back in the briefing room. Archie comes in five minutes later, carrying a pile of paper to show me my work. I suddenly see the connection. All the time I was 'flying', the simulator was drawing my track.

We compare the tracks to the patterns we drew earlier and I am given some hints and tips for day two, before I am dismissed for the day. That wasn't too bad a start! Long may it continue!

As I get back to the country house, Alison and Jo are keen to know how I got on. It's a bit like coming home from school and telling your parents about your day, which I think is quite funny really, bearing in mind I left school twenty five years ago. Then again, it's quite nice to have someone to talk to. I didn't have that in the hotel.

The rest of the week passes in a similar fashion. New exercises are added every day and my sessions in the simulator get slightly longer.

Everything seems to be put together in a logical fashion and, although I am working hard, I am not finding it too taxing. I see now what Archie meant when he said this course would be more organised, and of course doing everything full time is really helping. That said, the fact that my time here is limited does niggle me occasionally.

Week two goes by in a flash, and before I know it, I have had the usual hectic weekend at home and find myself in week three.

It isn't until the end of week four, however, that Archie decides it's time to take my training to the next level.

'You have flown the aeroplane and you have flown the syllabus,' he sums up, 'now it's time to put the two together. From next Monday, you will be flying everything in the Duchess.'

I am looking forward to it the whole weekend. If I make the same progress in the aeroplane that I have made in the simulator, it will be a question of three weeks at most, and I'm done, early enough to keep the stress levels down and hopefully have a little holiday before I go back to Stansted. In fact, a holiday is long overdue!

As I turn up for my flight on Monday afternoon, things do not look quite as rosy. The whole morning the wind has been increasing, and now it is beginning to reach storm force. I don't suppose we are going to go flying in this, not on my 'first day'.

Archie has different ideas. 'Yes, it is getting worse,' he admits, 'but it is still flyable and I think we should give it a go.'

Far be it from me to argue with the instructor, so I commence my pre-flight work, albeit with a heavy heart. I cannot think of a way of getting out of this without looking like a complete wimp! Well, if I'm going for it, I'm going for it properly!

Half an hour later we are sitting at the holding point for runway 26, listening to air traffic's broadcasts of ever increasing wind speeds. The little Duchess is moving and shaking as if we were airborne already, and I am getting more and more apprehensive. Not that I am worried that anything serious might happen. I just have the feeling that I am not going to have a very good flight here, but Archie is still confident that we should go and busies himself putting up the screens to block out my view, in order to simulate the foggy flying conditions I am supposed to be coping with. All I am left with is a little window that allows me to catch a glimpse of the runway for take-off. Once airborne, that, too, will be closed.

I do not want to look like a chicken and make my way onto the runway.

'Clear for take-off,' come the instructions from the tower.

Now I am committed. I move the throttles forward and go. Whatever happens, I best do what I always do and decide to not be fazed by the weather. I imagine that I have 200 people behind me waiting to go on holiday, who are relying on the cool professionals at the front. Off we go.

When I am first in the air, things do not seem too bad. It is bumpy but manageable. I decide I must have played my usual trick and worried about nothing. We make our way over to Southampton and try a few manoeuvres.

It's a struggle. It seemed so easy in the simulator, but the techniques I used there do not seem to work here today. I get more and more frustrated.

'Let's go back to Bournemouth,' Archie suggests as he probably feels I am not learning anything. As we approach Bournemouth, the wind has strengthened even more.

We are all over the place and I find it impossible to control the aeroplane, never mind produce any worth while results.

I suddenly find myself feeling something I have not yet felt during a flying lesson. Fear! Sheer undisguised fear! I am not admitting it of course, I just carry on. But, unfortunately with the fear another feeling manifests itself – airsickness.

I cannot believe it! I have never been airsick in my life! I never even considered the possibility. And now here I am, scared and sick, but I am not going to show it. We'll be on the ground soon. In a few minutes this will be over and I can put a line under it and start again tomorrow.

Ohmygod, I'm feeling worse, and we still have another ten minutes or so to go, as we have about sixty knots of wind on the nose, slowing our progress to a snail's pace.

'Are you all right?' questions Archie.

By now I am white as a sheet and sweating like a pig. Oh Christ! 'You have control,' I just about manage under my breath as I reach for a sick bag.

Archie is reasonably sympathetic. He proceeds to take down the screens so I get a view of the country side below, which he is hoping will stop me throwing up. But it's too late! I'm on a roll. Archie is flying the aeroplane whilst I fill the first sick bag, and then a second. Oh great! I'll never live this down.

The approach into Bournemouth is not helping. The Duchess jolts and shudders and is upright one minute and sideways the next. Things are getting worse near the ground, and all the while I'm filling sick bags. Eventually the runway, only visible through the side window minutes earlier, appears in the front windscreen and Archie manages a perfect landing despite the weather.

As we taxi in to park, I hold on to my sick bags like some sort of trophy. I am unable to speak. I cannot remember ever having felt so embarrassed in my life! I just want to find a hole and hide in it.

We walk back to the class room and I quickly dispose of the sick bags, but not before they've been noticed by some of the other students. Can this get any worse?!

I check my face in the mirror. It can safely be said that I am no longer pale, as I am now bright red, and that includes the whites of my eyes! I decide to take cover in the briefing room.

Lucy joins me twenty minutes later carrying a cup of tea.

'Hey don't worry,' she reassures me. 'You weren't the first and you won't be the last.'

'But I am NEVER airsick normally,' I protest, trying to maintain some form of dignity.

'Yes, but it is pretty wild out there, and don't forget you had the screens up, which a lot of students find difficult at first, but they normally get used to it pretty quickly.'

I am still not convinced. What if I am the stupid one, who does not get used to it, and I will have spend all that money and I will have achieved nothing.

It's as if Lucy is guessing my thoughts. 'Let me tell you, we had one chap last year, brilliant pilot, but suffered tremendously with airsickness. No matter what he tried, nothing would cure it. Give him a few bumps in the air on a sunny day and it was Niagara Falls! He even managed to throw up all over Archie on the day of his dress rehearsal test, as it were. Still, he went on the next day and passed his test first time, and now he flies for British Airways.'

I must admit that story does go some way towards restoring my equilibrium. I just hope the winds die down tomorrow.

On Tuesday the winds have indeed died down and I can't wait to get airborne. I must do well today and nip last night's confidence crisis in the bud.

As I find myself airborne with Archie yet again, I am still not finding it as easy as flying the simulator, but compared to yesterday it's a piece of cake.

I manage a hold over Southampton followed by an approach to the airport. Just as I get low enough to land, Archie instructs me to climb away again, for another hold and approach at Bournemouth. This time we do land and soon find ourselves back in the briefing room.

'I think what you did there could legally be called a holding pattern,' concludes Archie, 'albeit only just.'

I take that as a compliment. Compared to yesterday I had a good day out, and not a sick bag in sight!

During the rest of the week I get airborne twice a day. In the morning I travel in the back and observe my fellow students, in the afternoon I have my own lesson, usually accompanied by one or two people in the back observing me. This way we can all learn from each other's mistakes. It's like having two lessons for the price of one.

Slowly I am finding my pace. I manage to produce more accurate results and am showing steady progress at last. I am still a long way from test standard, but Rome wasn't built in a day either. As long as I get things together in my eight weeks, I'll be just fine.

The weather is rougher on some days than others but I am pleased to say that my airsickness seems to be a thing of the past. If I hadn't gone up on that fateful day with the crazy winds, it would never have happened at all, I'm sure.

Week five is soon over and week six goes by in a similar fashion. I feel more and more confident when I find myself in week seven, where we concentrate on my weak points in order to 'iron them out' as Archie puts it.

He must be good at ironing, as on Wednesday arrangements are made for me to take my pre-test the following Friday. This will be my dress rehearsal and my last chance to make mistakes before the real thing. Mess up the pre-test and it's no big deal. Mess up the real thing and risk professional and financial ruin. I feel ready.

The Thursday before is a day off to recover, a chance to go out and look at the country side. I decide to drive to the seafront and enjoy the sunshine. As far as I remember the best views in Bournemouth are from Hengistbury Head, a spit of land, strictly speaking belonging to the nearby town of Christchurch, but that's by the by.

I pull into the car park and am amazed at how busy it is, even at the end of February. I decide to scramble up to the top of the hill and take a look at the bay, before walking back down the easy way and then making my way along the seafront.

The beach, sheltered from the wind today, is full of people. There are some children playing in the sand, some older kids flying kites, and there are hardly any spare tables at the café. I decide to sit on the patio and order a drink.

Five minutes later the best hot chocolate I have ever seen is put in front of me: A huge mug, full of thick chocolate with marshmallows, topped with a generous amount of whipped cream. Mmmm! 'It's a meal in itself' I think as I give in to my sweet tooth.

Life is good really. Here I am, sitting by the seaside, sipping my drink, seemingly without a care in the world. Yes, the imminent conclusion of my course does play on my mind, but today I am making a special effort not to think about it. Today is a day to relax. Sometimes it's good to get away – it's like a mini holiday. Tomorrow will be a different matter.

I must have been sitting there for half an hour and my cold bum now reminds me that it is only February after all. It's time to make a move. I get up to pay my bill, which is when it happens:

An excruciating pain tears through my lower back and for a second I am unable to move. I slowly lower myself back onto the chair and look around, embarrassed. Nobody is watching. Oh good, I try again and manage to get up this time hanging on to the table for dear life, but it is impossible to stand. With a thud I slump back onto my chair.

Oh well, this is going to be interesting. I know immediately that my problem is harmless but unfortunately debilitating. I have had back trouble before, on several occasions, and have been doing regular exercises to keep it at bay. Of course recently, with everything else going on, I have been neglecting them a bit. That, in combination with the stresses of the last few weeks and of course the cold chair – I had it coming!

But never mind that! The question is what on Earth am I going to do next? If I could try again, very slowly to get up, I might just manage to somehow hobble back to the car, and once there I can formulate some sort of plan. I pull myself up and ... no it's no good. I'm going to need some help here.

There is no point ringing an ambulance – my condition is not that serious. All I really need is a hand from a friend. I consider my options.

Five minutes later I am explaining my dilemma to Alison on the phone.

'Don't worry, we are on our way,' Alison reassures me and half an hour later they are joining me on the patio of the beach café and are making joined efforts to get me to stand up.

They manage it eventually and I am able to walk, very very slowly, back to my car.

'Are you sure you don't want to go to hospital?' Jo's face shows a crease of concern.

'Really, not,' I almost beg them. 'There'll be absolutely nothing they can do. This will sort itself out, within a few days.'

Jo drives me back in my own car, whilst Alison follows in theirs. We seem to be in the famous Bournemouth rush-hour by now, and the journey seems endless.

As we pull up on drive at last, I only just manage to scramble out of the car and hobble upstairs to my room. There is no relief from the pain. Sitting does not help, nor does lying down. The only thing that will help here is regular doses of ibuprofen and time, the one commodity I am now running out of!

I pick up the phone and call 'Professional Flyers' to explain my dilemma..

Paula cannot believe what she is hearing. 'Are you jinxed or something?' she wants to know.

'Hopefully not, it's nothing serious really,' I reassure her. 'Just a total pain in the ... well, the back, I suppose. And, obviously I'll be unable to fly tomorrow.... Yes, I'll give you a call at the beginning of the week to tell you how I'm doing..... Yes, thanks.'

I put the phone down.

There is no way I can go home this weekend and endure a three-hour-drive, let alone cope with the house work the other end.

I come to an arrangement with Alison about weekend lodgings, food supplies and the use of the washing machine. As always she is most accommodating.

On Sunday afternoon I am feeling mildly better, but there is still no way I can drive a car, never mind fly an aeroplane.

And this is it of course, this is week eight! At the beginning of week nine, I am supposed to be back at Stansted. So I have one week, five days to be precise to recover, deliver a reasonable performance in the rehearsal test despite the break, and then actually go and pass my test – that's quite a tall order.

'Near impossible,' says Archie with emphasis as I phone up on Monday morning. 'The stress of time pressure alone will be enough to mess things up. You need to find more time, at least another week, to make this happen. There is too much at stake here to take any risks.' He is adamant and he is right of course.

But more time?! How on Earth am I going to find more time?

The episode where we reach a conclusion

By Monday morning I have a plan. I must ring my boss, Ian, at Stansted and throw myself at his mercy. There is no other way, if I want to both finish this course *and* keep my job.

'Ah, this is most irregular,' is the reply as I explain my story ten minutes later. 'We have already made an exception for you to let you take all your leave at the same time, and now you are asking for more?'

I thought he would say that, and I have prepared a counter argument: 'I am fully aware that I am not entitled to anymore favours,' I remark. 'However, I went to all this trouble to finish a project and got so close to doing just that, when a last minute hiccup spoilt my plans. This is an expensive venture which I am not prepared to leave unfinished. I am aware of my duty and I will be back at work if you insist. But I would then come down here, on every set of days off, in order to finish my course.'

The phone on the other end has gone silent. I can virtually see Ian scratching his beard.

'Very well then, let me think about it,' he eventually concludes.

That's better than a 'no'. I spend the rest of the day glued to my phone, until it rings again at four p.m... It's Ian.

'We've thought about it,' he begins, 'and we have come to the conclusion that we want a relaxed controller back on the watch, who is going to concentrate on the task in hand. We are not going to have that if all you can think about is how to get back to Bournemouth to finish your damn course. So here's the deal. You can have another two weeks' leave, but they will have to be unpaid. Also, please be aware that this is it; you will be back at work on March 25th, full of your usual enthusiasm, come hell or high water. Am I making myself clear?'

'Yes, thank you, I mean, perfectly, yes, thank you, well ah.... Good bye,' I stutter as the relief is flooding through me!

By Wednesday I am well enough to drive the car, and I make my way down to the airport, to attempt a little revision lesson. To my surprise, getting in and out of the aeroplane is the hardest bit. Once in it I seem to be able to fly okay.

On Thursday I am virtually back to normal and have another flight which sees me back at normal standard. Archie is pleased.

'The pre-test is booked for Monday,' he informs me. At first I am disappointed that we cannot do it Friday, but on the other hand it's good to have another day at home this weekend, after last week's fiasco! I decide to relax and have my weekend, before attacking week nine with renewed enthusiasm.

As I am on the motorway once again on Sunday night, direction Bournemouth, I feel quietly confident. All I have to do tomorrow is to produce a normal flight, without too many stupid things in it, and they probably let me have a go at the real thing.

I cannot deny that I feel a little nervous on Monday morning, but I am so keen to bring this course to some sort of conclusion, it is mind over matter.

This time I am not flying with Archie. The school want to see an independent assessment and have therefore given me an instructor who has not seen me fly before. I am given my route and my aeroplane and am sitting in the briefing room taking care of the usual flight preparation. Forty minutes later I report ready to Dennis Evans who is going to fly with me today.

We spend two hours in the air, and Dennis puts me through my paces. We leave Bournemouth to fly to Bristol, where I am flying a hold and then an approach to the airport. Everything has to be accurate. A little bit to the right or to the left of my track, a little bit too high or too low – and we are looking at disaster! It would be hard enough just to fly the aeroplane, but I am responsible for the radio as well as well as a number of checks that have to be performed at a regular basis, to make sure that all is well.

In the beginning I went off my heading every time I pressed the radio button, but not today. I am concentrating very hard indeed! We leave Bristol and practice the usual emergencies, then make our way back to Bournemouth, where Dennis promptly declares me fit for test.

I am so happy I have passed my 'dress rehearsal' that I do not even spare one tiny thought for the real event tomorrow. That's probably not a bad thing!

I awake Tuesday morning, after a good night's sleep and sit down to a hearty breakfast. My test won't be until the afternoon, so there is no point getting nervous just yet, surely.

After breakfast I spend a little bit of time having one last look at my notes and at all the hints and tips I have been given over the last few weeks. Finally I decide I can do no more.

I put on my shirt and tie and make my way to the airport picking up a cheese sandwich on the way. I might not feel like eating later on, but I am keen not to fly on an empty stomach. I don't want anything to affect my concentration levels.

On my arrival it's just a run-in-the-mill day at 'Professional Flyers' and I try and revel in the normal atmosphere, joking with the other students and eventually scoffing my cheese sandwich.

I have imagined this day many times over during my training here, and I have always expected myself to be a bundle of nerves. But to my own surprise, I seem to be quite calm and resigned to the task ahead, which is completely out of character. Let's hope it stays this way.

At half past twelve I'm on my way to the test centre. Lucy is giving me last minute tips in the car, and I must admit that I am currently more concerned about her driving than I am about my test. In the three miles from the school to the test centre, she has managed to overtake two lorries in the most impossible places, ignore bicycles and has generally driven like a hooligan. Her style does definitely not match her otherwise professional demeanour and catches me by surprise. Oh well, I'll soon be in the safest form of transport.

My test begins in the briefing room of the test centre, where I am given my route and forty-five minutes to do the planning. It's the same thing as every day, just in unfamiliar surroundings.

At 2pm 'Exam 09' is cleared for take-off. 'So this is it', I think to myself as I am rolling down the runway.

Any further thinking is strictly confined to the exercise, which takes us North at first, then West along the airway, and eventually South along another airway down to Exeter. Exeter is jokingly known as the 'black run', the difficult one, as some radio beacons are in a less than ideal position, giving this particular destination an extra edge. But I have been there twice before, and I made all my stupid mistakes then, so I am quietly confident.

On reaching Exeter I am not taking any chances. I cannot afford to be messed around by air traffic control. I'd sooner get in there first and tell them what we need to do.

'Exeter Radar, exam 09, I have my training requirements when you are ready to copy.'

'P..P..Pass your message,' the controller is somewhat surprised at my assertiveness.

I tell him what we need to do and he obliges. 'Take up the hold at the beacon', he instructs.

I now have to quickly form a picture in my head as to where I am in relation to that beacon. There are three different ways to join a holding pattern; I must pick the correct entry in order to pass my test. I look at my instruments and make a decision.

Once around the hold, I am cleared for the approach, my clue to leave the hold, again in the correct way and fly along the pattern, whilst deciding upon a sensible rate of descend. If I do not follow the pattern correctly, or descend at the wrong point or at the wrong rate, I will find myself flying home, £1000 worse off, and with nothing to show for it. The pressure is indescribable, but now is not the time to think about it. I concentrate on the task in hand.

The approach is looking good. I fly down to my decision point. In real life I would decide here whether to land (if I can see the runway) or to climb away (if I cannot). For the purposes of this test, the decision is made for me. I am to pretend that I cannot see the runway. I push the throttles forward and climb away.

'Time for the emergencies,' I think, and I am not to be disappointed as miraculously one of my engines fails. As the aeroplane yaws to the left, I quickly take the necessary action. For the next twenty minutes or so we will be flying on one engine, but I must maintain the same accuracy.

The engine gets restarted and we are on our way back to Bournemouth. We go through another batch of emergencies on the way, but it's nothing I haven't seen before. I am quite calm now – things are going well and my confidence is growing by the minute.

Soon we are making our way back to Bournemouth for another hold followed by another approach, this time all on one engine. Again, I go down to my decision point, then apply power to climb away, this time into the visual traffic pattern around the airport. I am working hard to keep the aircraft in the right place, maintaining a good lookout and listening to the instructions from the tower.

The airport is very busy, as we are flying the final bits of the test. I am almost done now, and am just performing the last of my pre landing checks. All the checks are mnemonics, and you just say them out aloud and do them at the same time, whilst of course flying the aeroplane and listening to the radio.

As I am coming in to land, I am being squeezed in between two airliners. I have never been asked to 'speed up' on final approach before and then to 'vacate the runway at the first available exit'.

So, I'm faster *and* I have to come off quicker. So, I will need to brake harder when I land. How much harder, I have no idea, but I am not taking any chances.

I touch down and stand on the brakes. Everything that's on the back seat hits the wind screen, including a packet of mints, which promptly bursts open and scatters its contents all over the dashboard. As I take the tight turn off the runway, all the mints are in one corner. Oh sh***t!

I taxi off in silence. 'I have control,' demands the examiner.

Ohmygod! I so frightened him with that arrival, he doesn't even trust me to taxi now. I brace myself for the worst.

'Congratulations you have just passed your test!'

Did he just say pass? 'Pardon?' I say. I need to hear this again!

'Y o u h a v e j u s t p a s s e d y o u r t e s t !'

Christ! I have done it! I have passed first time! This will take a while to sink in.

After the debrief, I am invited to sit and wait in the cafeteria of the test centre. I cannot help overhearing the examiner on the phone to my school.

'Yes, you'd better pick her up. I think she is somewhere up a lamp post.'

That night we are celebrating in the pub, as of course, is the school's tradition. I remember being here not so long ago, when Sandy passed, and here I am again, and today is about me! We have dinner and plenty to drink, quite possibly too much to drink, but this time I manage not to get banned from the pub. Still, the hangover has its moments, and it will take two days until I am able to tackle the journey home.

On Thursday morning I drive away from the country house, onto the forest road and up to the roundabout. I turn onto the ring road, and before I know it I am on the motorway heading for Stansted.

I am driving along listening to the radio, and I realise that my face is wet and then I realise that I am crying. And then I cry properly, for a good twenty minutes, and I have no idea why, and when the crying stops I start smiling, and it would take weeks for that smile to fade.

For the first few days at home I feel a little bit out of sorts really. I am quite pleased I won't have to work for another five days. Over the past nine weeks, my 'new' way of life has become such a habit that it feels quite strange to be at home. On top of that I have a rotten cold! It must be all the stress coming out.

By the weekend I am feeling more like my old self again. I am even looking forward to going back to work, which is what I do, on Tuesday morning, carrying the obligatory packet of doughnuts by means of celebration.

Apart from that I want as little fuss as possible. Best to just keep my head down and get on with the job as I promised.

Getting back into the Stansted ways is harder than I thought. Not only have I lost the edge a little bit during my ten week absence, I keep confusing the airport with Bournemouth and am sending all the aircraft to holding points that do not actually exist at Stansted. I'm going to have to knuckle down here.

Two days later though, it's as if I have never been away. My colleagues, who have had to supervise my work since I am officially a student, think that I have settled in enough to take my exams again, which are scheduled for the Thursday after.

I don't feel so much nervous but slightly apprehensive as our local examiner sits down next to me to watch me in action.

Two hours later we are downstairs, where I am bombarded with questions to ensure that I have not forgotten any rules. The questions are more for my benefit rather than exam purposes, and by the end of the shift on Thursday, I am signed off to work on my own again. I am pleased that it all went without a hitch, after all the favours I've been given.

Life soon settles back into its old routine, and it's time to think about the next step, the very last step, that needs to be completed before I can finally go job hunting.

The episode where multi-tasking is taken to a new level

So far all my flying efforts have essentially been down to me. I had to fly, find my way round and talk to ATC. The commercial world, however, believes that the tasks in the cockpit should be shared, and this team work, with its own set of rules, will take some getting used to.

Therefore, one last course will have to be mastered. Thankfully it will only last ten days, and thankfully it has none of the stress levels associated with the IR course, but (and this is a big but), I have no hope in hell of getting another ten days off before January, unpaid or otherwise, and no way can my job hunting wait that long!

Well, if I cannot work around a course, maybe I have to find a course that can work around me ...

At first I am getting nowhere fast. Every training establishment I contact insist I attend *one* course, from start to finish. Finally though, I come across a brand new school in Leeds, who are prepared to offer a more flexible approach.

'It's is not what people usually do, but I can see your predicament,' says Julie, the school secretary, in answer to my question. 'Just let me make a few enquiries.'

Later that afternoon, Julie returns my call. 'Well, they are quite happy for you to do your course in bits during the theory part,' she explains, 'as long as you can attend the flying segment in one go.'

'How long is the flying segment?' I want to know.

'Five days training, without a test at the end, you'll be pleased to know.'

Well, I am pleased to know that there is no test, less pleased to find out I have to attend five days in a row. But far be it from me to question a compromise.

'Done,' I say cheerfully and dig out my credit card to pay the fee. 'When can I start?'

Julie suggests a few dates and we compare diaries. I get four days off in a row at Stansted, the first one is after a night shift, which means I don't wake up until lunch time really, but again I could sleep in my break at work, skip the morning's sleep and just accept I'll be a bit tired for the day. I've done it before when I went on holiday.

We pick a few dates, and Julie is even able to offer accommodation in a little B&B just off the airport. I am sorted. I'll be starting on Monday.

On Sunday night I go to work, with my usual night shift gear, plus a suitcase for four days in Leeds. I am quite excited really. Here is another adventure coming up.

My enthusiasm is waning slightly, however, as I find myself on the M11 the next morning, at the start of the rush hour, trying to keep my eyes open after just three hours of sleep at work. It's seven a.m. and I have to be there for eleven. I keep sipping on my can of red bull, as I am crawling towards Cambridge.

There I interrupt my journey for breakfast and a huge cup of coffee, and as I find myself on the A14, the traffic has died down a bit and I am making progress. Soon I am at Peterborough and am making my way up the A1. I'm not even that tired anymore.

I reach Leeds-Bradford airport at a quarter past eleven. Everything was running on time until I hit the city bypass. There the traffic almost stopped, due to an unfortunate combination of traffic lights and roundabouts. How can you have an airport which is not on a major road?! Well, at least I'm here now.

I settle into the classroom at Leeds Professional Training and try and pay as much attention as possible. To be perfectly honest, though, I can't wait to have a lunch time nap.

No chance of that, as at lunch time the group gather in the local pub. Oh well, that'll save going out in the evening then, and I can just *sleep*.

At five p.m. we get to leave the classroom. I must say I am quite impressed so far. It must have been very interesting.

I take my hat off to the tutor, who must have been good to keep me awake.

My B&B is literally around the corner from the airport. I have taken a bit of a gamble here with my accommodation and am relieved when I find the place clean and tidy. Gwen, the landlady shows me to my room.

I'm on the third floor, under the roof. The room is tiny but comfortable, with pine furniture and thick curtains to block out the light for the shift workers. Gwen tells me she has people in from the airport all the time, appreciates shift patterns, and offers continental breakfast around the clock.

As I unpack my mini suitcase, I can hardly keep my eyes open. It is eight p.m. and still daylight, when I give in to the land of nod.

Eleven hours later the world looks a different place. I am wide awake and looking forward to breakfast. I won't have to be at the school until ten. Oh bliss!

Day two, three and four are over before I know it, and at five p.m. on Thursday I hit the motorway, direction Stansted. That's four days down, three to go, plus the five days flying. Oh well, it's manageable.

It's almost ten o'clock when I pull onto my drive back in Bishop's Stortford. I managed to have dinner along the way and all I have to do now is fall into bed, so I can get up for my morning shift tomorrow.

The next days off are a much more sedate affair, as thankfully they do not tie up with the continuation of the course. I make a point of being around and meet up with a few of my colleagues from work. Not a word about my efforts up North, obviously. It'll all be done and dusted soon.

The break after that ties in beautifully with day five to seven of my course, and so I find my self travelling back to Leeds. This time thankfully, it's only three days of lessons, so I get to sleep first.

I find myself back in the classroom, with a new set of fellow students, and back in Gwen's B&B. Everything goes without a hitch this time. The theory over with, it's time to formulate a plan on how to attend five days in a row for the flying part in the simulator.

Julie comes to the rescue. 'The flying is round the clock shift work,' she explains, 'four hours at a time, make that six hours including the briefing sessions. Knowing your predicament with work, lets roster you in first, to make sure you can attend all the sessions.'

There is definitely a box of chocolates on its way to Julie here. That's for sure. She's been a brick!

Together we formulate a plan which works very well in theory, but will take three weeks to put into practice, as my days off at work will have to tie in with the flying programme.

Eventually we find a slot in May. I will have to drive up again after my last night shift (red bull and coffee at the ready), crash out in the B&B and go in the simulator late that night. That will be followed by another two late slots on days off two and three, and then a lunch time slot on day four, leaving me time to drive home again to do my morning shift the next day. That shift will finish at two, after which I will need to drive up again for an evening slot on day five, and I'll be done. It's a tall order, but it's the only way to finish the course.

The programme works but is exhausting. That said I am well settled into my mini routine by day two. I go off to the simulator at ten pm, and am home again at three in the morning. Good job I'm used to shift work. My sim partner Max does not enjoy the late nights but feels he should get used to them, as he is about to start work for a cargo airline.

On day three I am woken up rudely by an almighty crash downstairs.. At first I cannot make out what has happened, then I realise that there must have been some sort of accident.

I quickly get dressed and make my way to the kitchen, where I find Gwen sitting at the kitchen table, in a state of deep distress.

'It's Paul,' she exclaims, 'he's only fallen off the ladder – I think he's broken his leg.'

I peep around the corner and there is Gwen's husband, on the conservatory floor, holding his leg in agony.

'Ambulance is on its way,' he reassures me, 'one minute I was putting up blinds, next minute I'm on t'floor.'

Gwen seems to be more upset than Paul, and I make her a cup of tea to calm her down, until the ambulance arrives.

The paramedics take no chances. Paul is being taken to hospital and Gwen is going with him. I promise to keep an eye on things until they are back.

They are gone for hours. By the time they return I have walked the dog and have produced some sort of dinner. I am just putting the finishing touches to the gravy, when a taxi pulls up outside.

'He's only gone and broken his leg,' exclaims Gwen as Paul hobbles through the front door, sporting a plaster cast. 'Six weeks in plaster they said, what is going to happen to the B&B, with our son away on holiday an' all?'

'When is your son coming back?' I want to know as we are sitting down for dinner.

'Not for another week,' replies Gwen, 'and what with all the fetching and carrying, and with me not being able to drive, and with him not being able to do a thing,' she trails off, threatening to burst into tears again.

'I can drive,' the words come out before I can stop them. (What – am I mad – have I just offered to run a B&B here, on top of all my other troubles?)

But I am sorry for Gwen and I could help out a little bit, just for the next two days, until I go home again. I have no idea what needs doing, but they'll be able to tell me that.

I ask Paul to make a list of things they need, and that very evening Gwen and I are off to the Cash & Carry. We spend about an hour loading our trolley up with everything that the two of them might need for their business venture, until their son returns from holiday on Wednesday.

It takes us another half hour to unload the car and put things away. Gwen is quite happy to take it from there, and I am off to the simulator. Max will be here within the hour to give me a lift.

There isn't quite so much spare time on day four, as my training session starts at two p.m., but I pop across to the supermarket, so Gwen can have another little shop. That should see them through until their son returns from holiday. As I leave the B&B that evening for the last time, Gwen is immensely grateful.

'Thank you so much, love, I don't know what we would have done without you.'

She gives me the card for the B&B for future reference and I am on my way, first to the airport and then to drive home.

I must admit I haven't had a dull moment in the last few weeks. I quite look forward to my leisurely drive home, with my dinner in the middle.

By the time I get home it's one a.m., leaving me just five hours sleep before I have to get up for my morning shift, followed, of course, by yet another drive up North for my final day of the course.

This crazy schedule is beginning to take its toll. I am dog tired the next morning. I will just about find the energy to complete my shift, my drive and my course today, but I really cannot see how I'm supposed to drive home again after that and then go to work for yet another early shift. I need to try and sort something out – and fast!

Luckily I find a volunteer who will swap shifts with me, so that tomorrow has become an afternoon duty. I will still have to drive home, but at least I get to have a lie-in and some recovery time.

Even more luckily he doesn't ask too many questions either. 'Out on the tiles again midweek? You are such a party animal! You really want to stop burning the candle at both ends you know.'

I assume a suitably guilty expression, get in my car and drive back to Leeds.

Twelve hours later I leave Leeds Professional training, clutching my course certificate. Well, that's done at last.

The drive home seems to last forever. I am so tired; I can hardly keep my eyes open. I have tried red bull and coffee and all sorts of tricks but it's no good. As I pass Newark my eye lids feel like lead and I realise I am getting onto dangerous territory. I make the sensible decision and stop at the local Travelodge.

Not that I am prepared for a night stop, but who cares. I can sort myself out in the morning once I'm back home. Good job I've got the morning off!

I wake up midmorning, completely disorientated. Oh well, at least I have missed the traffic chaos. It doesn't take long to whizz down the motorway towards Stansted. What a difference it makes when you are awake!

I get home at midday and am on my way to work at one. All I want to do now is go to work and then go home, like a normal person. And then, when I've recovered, on the days off maybe, I can finally start job-hunting!

The episode where I need to escape

So, here we go. I feel cheerful as I tap away on the keyboard, creating a CV that I feel will stand out with a potential employer. There are so many unwritten rules:

True to life of course, but no longer than one page. Do not use crazy colours and include a good photo.

Good job I went to the photographers especially. Photo booths always make me look as if I have just escaped from a mental institution, probably not the image any airline would be after.

By the afternoon I have produced a CV that matches all the above requirements, yet will hopefully stand out for the paper it is printed on: an understated cream coloured expensive affair that will hopefully turn out to be worth every penny.

Now - airlines to apply for - well, every single one, obviously. A foot in the door, any door, is everything, and beggars can't be choosers. If sceptics are to be believed, I have very little chance of finding a job at all, due to the age / training risk connection.

On the up side, I did pass all my tests first time, as I have indeed done all my life, got very high pass marks and never stopped learning since I left school.

According to the experts, however, once you hit forty, all that counts for nothing, as your brain will miraculously shrink to nothing and you suddenly turn into a bumbling stumbling idiot that barely knows how to spell aviation, never mind fly an aeroplane. That attitude firmly puts me into the 'beggar' category.

Well, we'll see about that! If I apply to everybody, once a month or so, then by law of averages, somebody somewhere will eventually give me an interview, followed hopefully by a job, and one job is all I need.

I spend the rest of the afternoon composing application letters to go with my CV. Apparently airlines get thousands of uninvited applications every day, and whether yours is actually read or not depends more on luck than anything else.

By the end of the week I have written and posted over fifty applications.

Two weeks later my first reply arrives: '... thank you once again for your interest in ABC airlines and good luck in your chosen career'

A couple of days later another two replies arrive, more or less of the same wording.

Oh, well. No point in giving up at the first hurdle! I shall just have to apply again at the end of the month.

I fine tune my CV and my application letters and try the whole thing again in July, with the exact same result. The same happens in August, and in September I get no replies at all.

Not that I am entitled to a reply exactly. I mean I am effectively 'cold-calling', and if people choose to ignore my efforts, there is no point in taking it personally. It's just so damn frustrating, that's all, even more so considering that one by one, my fellow course students are landing interviews. It's largely a case of who you know, not what you know, they claim.

I decide to become better at networking. A couple of pilots I know at Stansted promise to hand in my application form to *the right person*. I feel hopeful for a while until this, too, comes to nothing.

In October, I receive an e-mail saying that I have been short listed for an interview with a well-known local airline. I can hardly contain my excitement! This is it! This has got to be it! The e-mail suggests there might be a several month wait, but it will happen eventually.

Since the day I got my letter, I have been glued to my mobile. During the next couple of months I refuse to be parted with it. It's on at work which is very much frowned upon, it's on all night, and on one sorry occasion I am thrown out of the cinema for refusing to switch it off. Yet, the precious phone call never comes.

Other people I know to be in the same position seem to get called, and I find myself constantly trying to work out, why it hasn't been my turn yet and when my turn would come. I can think of very little else. I am obsessed!

By January I have had no success whatsoever. Meanwhile the entire bunch of people I met at 'Professional Flyers' seem to have either found a job, or at least have some interviews in the pipeline. Yes, most of them are at least ten years younger than me, but surely this can't be it. There must be something I am doing wrong.

Surely in the end, my iron determination will help me succeed. It's getting harder and harder to hang on to that belief, though, as more and more rejection letters drop on to my doorstep.

What makes me feel worse is that I am not flying enough. The odd hour of flying instructing here and there is hardly going to keep me current in all those procedures required to be flown with an airline.

Yet I am working like a one-armed paper hanger. If I'm not at work, I am flying instructing or writing job applications. A holiday is out of the question, there isn't any leave left. What I need is a weekend away, some days off to think and evaluate where I am going here.

After some consideration I decide on a few days in Lincolnshire. I have always enjoyed the countryside up there, with its flatlands and its windmills and its dykes, just like in Holland. That's what I need, a complete change of scenery and a little B&B, way off the beaten track.

As I pack my car for the three days away, I feel happier already. In got the walking boots and the bad weather gear. The job applications can stay behind! Soon I am back on the M11, heading north, this time strictly for pleasure and fun! Little do I realise that it would be this very trip which would turn my luck around.

It's a beautiful March morning. I leave the M11, enter the A14 and then follow the A1 up to Peterborough. From there it's just forty minutes to Spalding. Last time I came up here I stayed at Wisbech and did some walking around there, but according to the guide books Spalding is more beautiful. I am not disappointed.

I park the car in the market square and have a look around. I see a tiny little town centre, with a small selection of shops, and not just one but four bakeries. The pedestrian area is busy with Saturday shoppers who are strolling along the rows of market stalls, clearly enjoying the early spring sunshine.

I pop into the tourist information to see what else is on offer, pick up a few leaflets, and finally sit down in one of the bakeries, to enjoy a coffee and formulate some sort of plan.

'Riverboat trips' is catching my eye. The little stream I saw earlier must be bigger than I thought!

As I am queuing on the little jetty on Sunday morning, I realise that there are not one but two rivers, as well as the stream.

The little boat takes us along one of them, away from the town, through a bird sanctuary and finally stops at a retail outlet village. Shopping wasn't really part of the plan here, but I might as well have a quick look around, before I catch the next boat back again.

I nose around the row of shops, and finally come to a little park, the perfect lunch venue. I sit on a bench and scoff a sandwich, followed by a huge ice cream.

Just as I decide to wander back to the boat stop, I catch a glimpse of a hut in the corner of the park. It seems to be some sort of museum. Curiosity gets the better of me and I walk across to investigate.

It's a museum indeed inviting me in to 'experience the Fens'.

Oh well, it's always good to have a look at some local stuff, I think as I walk through the door and have a look around. Soon I find out that *a Fen is a piece of land that used to be water,* and I experience 'The Fens through the Ages', 'The Wildlife of the Fens' and finally 'The Fens today', before I pop out at the exit.

I decide to have a quick look at the display of postcards and local maps. Maybe I can find a perfect little walk for tomorrow. That is when I see it:

A bright and cheerful leaflet with pictures of the country side and '*See Lincolnshire from the Air' written* in big letters at the top. Of course! How could I not have realised! Fenmere airfield must be just around the corner. I remember flying there once, years ago, with a friend on one of our little daytrips, long before I even considered taking my commercial exams.

Now - this weekend, was meant to be strictly aviation-free. So really I should just walk away. But then, what is the harm of just having a little look at the tiny grass airfield this afternoon, just to watch a few aeroplanes and to have a coffee on the patio. I tuck the leaflet into my rucksack and make my way back to the boat stop.

As we moor at Spalding the sky has clouded over, and by the time I reach the car the first rain drops are starting to fall;

so much for the weather lasting the whole weekend! Never mind, I decide to pop in at Fenmere anyway. Now I have got my map I can see it is virtually on the way back to my B&B.

The airfield is tucked away in a farm lane, and by the time I spot it, I have almost driven past it. I stand on my brakes and screech into the entrance, park the car and make my way over to the clubhouse.

Most of the day's activities seem to be over thanks to the weather, and I have no problem finding a table. Oh well, I just have a quick coffee and then make my way back.

'I haven't seen you here before!' the voice that interrupts my thoughts belongs to a man in uniform, no doubt a flying instructor here at the club. 'Would normally be on my way home by now,' he continues, 'but the car packed up this morning, and the wife can't pick me up for another two hours. Would happen on a rainy afternoon where I finish early, wouldn't it?!'

I sympathise. 'Murphy's Law of aviation at its best,' I console him.

'Sounds like you are a flyer then,' says the man, who introduces himself as Leo.

He is obviously happy to chat, and over yet another coffee I give a brief account of my present situation. '... and so I decided to have a weekend away,' I finish, 'just to get away from the whole sorry mess.'

'Only to find yourself at a flying club,' counters Leo, 'and what does that tell you?' He continues to answer his own question. .'You obviously can't get away; you just have to find a way to make things happen'

I can see his logic. 'I just wish I knew how,' I respond, 'I am beginning to run out of ideas here.'

'You see, I have kind of the opposite problem,' continues Leo. I keep running out of flying instructors. One minute I take somebody on, the next minute they're off to fly for an airline and I'm back to square one again. Lost our Tom only this week, happy as we are for him to fly a big jet for Greek International Cargo. Don't suppose you fancy his job?'

I wasn't expecting that! 'You serious?' I don't know whether to be delighted or not as the practicalities of the whole scenario dawn on me. 'Well,' I eventually respond, 'I would. In fact I would be delighted. However I do live two hours drive away, and of course I would have to work part-time, around my shift pattern at work.'

'Too afraid to give up the day job, huh? Leo winks at me. How are you going to convince an airline that you are quite happy to pack in a sixty-grand-job where you are on top of the game, in order to be a trainee on about a third of the salary?'

I hadn't thought about it like that. May be Leo has got a point. I promise to think about it and be in touch.

A million different thoughts are going through my head as I am driving back to the B&B. I'm still all over the place at midnight. Thoughts are whirring through my head like out of control cogwheels. I have reached no conclusion whatsoever, as I sink into an exhausted sleep.

Monday morning dawns bright and beautiful – the perfect weather for my country walk. I am pleased. The walk will give me more thinking time.

After a substantial breakfast I check out of the B&B, don my walking boots and hit the country side.

Things are a little bit clearer in my head already. I mean what does the average airline entrant look like? Young, keen, possibly deeply in debt, with nothing to lose and everything to gain. Enthusiasm and dedication to the job are virtually guaranteed.

Then there is me: good job, comfortable house, good lifestyle. Would I be likely to go back to that lifestyle the minute things got tough in flying? I know I wouldn't, but that's not enough to convince a potential employer. I can suddenly see that, from an airline's point of view, I am possibly not such a good prospect.

It would be one thing to promise to give it all up for a flying job; it would be far more convincing to have done that already!

I play things through in my head. So far I have sold my sports car and replaced it with a more sedate and much cheaper vehicle. The house would have to go on the market anyway, to be replaced with a smaller home once I know where the job is taking me. Once it's sold there won't be any debts, in fact I have saved up a few pennies, in view of harder times to come, but to give up my job???

It would be the ultimate crazy step! So, worst case scenario, how long would I survive? I decide that, at a push, I could live on the pittance that is a flying instructor's pay for two years, all things considered. After that life would become exceedingly difficult. But if, after two years of giving it my all, I have still not found a job with an airline, it will probably time for a reality check and a return back to air traffic control.

So, in theory at least, it's possible. I'll just need to check a few details, before I can actually make up my mind.

Leo is surprised to hear from me so soon.

'Full-time from July will be fine,' he says, having realised I am on a three months' notice period, 'however, bearing in mind that's a long time away, I would need you to start part-time before then.'

We agree that I should spend two of my four days off at this school for now, starting from next month. He is even able to help out with accommodation, as a school friend of his is running a B&B down the road, which he insists is *the* place to stay around here. Oh well, it will do until I find a more permanent residence later on.

I am equally happy to find that I would probably be able to get my job back in the tower, should I really want to. During the following few days, I manage to speak to two people who have done just that. One girl had left for six months to travel around the world; the other one had tried her hand at flying a 757, which had then gone spectacularly wrong but I must not dwell on the negative here. The point is they both got their jobs back without too much trouble.

Ok, here goes then, here comes the boldest decision of my life!

The episode where I leave my comfort zone

Well, this is going to be a week and a half! Having made up my mind, I will now have to put my plan into action. Every bone in my body is telling me that I am crazy. I'm sure that, in years to come, I will remember this day where I was sitting in my cosy kitchen, taking positive steps to turn my life upside down.

First – the house. I am actually on my way to the estate agents now, to put it up for sale. I can honestly say that I feel sick to the pit of my stomach doing it. If there is a time to listen to the inner voice of reason, this is not it! I must close my eyes and carry on!

The estate agent is quite hopeful. 'Lots of enquiries for this sort of thing at the moment,' he reassures me, 'should get a good price.'

The surveyor, who comes round later that evening, confirms this opinion. Despite my constant remortgaging to afford my flying exams, I should still be left with a decent profit. That's good. I'm going to need that to support myself, and to afford further flying training with an airline, should I be lucky enough to actually find a job.

I must admit I have never been very lucky selling houses. Usually it takes me ages to get any viewings, and when I finally think I've found a buyer, they will drop out at the last minute, and drop me in it. Two of my neighbours have had their places on the market for over six months, and this doesn't bode well for a quick sale. Still, time will tell.

Despite my pessimism, I get a viewing the very next day. An elderly lady is looking for a place she does not have to decorate. She has already sold her place and is in a good position.

'She was very impressed,' I am informed by Colin, who has been busy marketing my house.

I should think so, too. I have spent the last five years decorating, and the house has not got a mark on it.

The very next day the phone rings again. It's Colin.

'Mrs Winton is back,' he sounds delighted, 'and she has asked for another viewing. This afternoon? Lovely.'

Gosh, this does sound good.

The next time I speak to Colin, he can hardly contain his excitement. 'She turned up with a *measuring tape,*' he squeals, 'went from room to room, measured everything and asked lots of questions.' Colin is brimming with optimism.

Well, the optimism turns out to be well placed, as the very next day Mrs Winton makes an offer, not just any offer, but the full asking price!

I cannot believe it! I have sold my house within 24 hours. This is not something I would have expected in my wildest dreams. Maybe it is a hint of fate telling me I am doing the right thing after all.

If I thought selling my house was hard, it was nothing compared to the next hurdle. This week I am going to have to resign from work. If I want to start full-time at Fenmere in July, I have two days left to do it in.

I write and re-write my letter of resignation. How can I just say 'thanks I resign', after fifteen years in a job I hugely enjoyed. How can I hint at possibly wanting to come back without looking like a total idiot for resigning in the first place?

Finally I write a version I am happy with. I decide to make an appointment with the boss, as I prefer to deliver the news in person.

I am quite nervous as I sit in the office at midday, dressed unusually smart in my suit, waiting for Ian to call me in. I hope this isn't too upsetting, as I shall have to work my afternoon shift. Well, whatever happens, I have given myself three hours to recover (and to have lunch).

I think Ian knows what is coming. I mean, it should hardly come as a huge surprise, bearing in mind all that has gone on in the previous months.

My thoughts are interrupted as the door opens and he beckons me into the office.

I hold up my letter and wait a few seconds for the penny to drop.

'What can I do you for?' asks Ian cheerfully and points me to a chair.

That went well!

'Well, the time has come for me to go and explore the flying side of the job,' I begin cautiously. 'This was never going to be an easy thing to do, but I'm afraid that in order to start flying in July, I am now forced to resign from my work here with effect from June 30th.'

'Lovely, thank you very much,' Alan takes the letter.

I am left standing there like a lemon. That is it? No 'good luck' or 'we are sorry to see you go'? Oh well, I shan't be missing his people skills!

He finally speaks. 'Pilots are such an unhappy bunch,' he says, 'most people I know that left here to go flying have come back. They all come back in the end.'

Well, thank you for those words of wisdom. Nothing like a bit of positive encouragement at times of crisis, albeit of the self-inflicted variety.

Time to go and have that lunch I think, as I politely take my leave and make my way to the terminal. I am going through the motions of ordering and eating a sandwich. It feels like all of this is happening to someone else and I am just a spectator.

I feel like I'm floating. Nothing seems real this week. Maybe I have a mental problem. I mean I don't feel as if I have a mental problem, but then mental patients don't, do they? They think the world is just fine and dandy, whilst it is obvious to everyone else that they are as mad as a bag of frogs!

I spend a short while looking around the shops, as this has always been an effective therapy against the blues, and indeed it is going a long way towards restoring my equilibrium.

By the time I sit down for a coffee I'm almost back to my normal self.

'Hey – flygirl!' I look around.

It's Dale, my Easyjet friend. Dale and I have known each other ever since he came for a visit in the tower, a couple of years ago. He knows all about my ambitions and has been a loyal and supportive friend. Dale has not had an easy time of it, either. An ex-navigator in the air force, he found himself on quite a steep learning curve when he first started flying commercially, plus he had a family to support.

'Have I got a story to tell you,' I begin as he joins me for a coffee.

Dale is all ears as I tell him about my week end away and the crazy decisions that followed.

Well, it's brave, I give you that,' he concludes, 'but at least you can never say you did not give it your all.'

I'm so glad I bumped into him! He is the first person in a long time that seems to understand my way of thinking. Maybe he's mad as well!

As I make my way back to the tower, I pick up a few doughnuts on the way, and decide to tell my colleagues the news.

'I didn't realise you had a job,' says Brian, my watch manager, 'who are you going to fly for?'

Ah, that. 'Well, I have a couple of options, so I haven't entirely decided,' is my evasive reply. I am just about hanging on to this today. If I tell people that I have just resigned in order to earn one fifth of my salary at a flying school, they will probably have me certified after all.

Then Brian does me a huge favour. 'Look, I don't know where you are going to live,' he says to me as we catch up in the break, 'but if you need an address and somewhere to store some furniture, you know I have a big house, don't you?'

I could kiss him! Even as an old friend he didn't have to do that. I am immensely grateful. The plan is to get rid of most of the furniture, and to put the rest into storage. This way I am not only going to save myself the storage costs, I also have a 'stable' address I can use on job applications, until I'm settled again.

Well, one more bunch of days off before I start instructing at Fenmere, all be it part-time initially. I will use this time to get organised and decide what to keep and what to let go.

Good job I have always detested clutter. It takes me the whole four days to sort out my stuff – it might have taken weeks otherwise! I decide to be ruthless. I'll keep my bed, my wardrobe, a table and chairs, my computer desk plus contents, that's it. That's enough to furnish a new place when I finally settle down somewhere. Things from Ikea are inexpensive enough should I want to add more furniture again later.

Most of my appliances will be sold with the house. Some of them are so old; they would probably not survive the move anyway. The rest of the furniture will be sold or given away! I have got weeks to do that.

The room at Fenmere will be furnished, so is my 'emergency accommodation' at Brian's. I am as organised as I can be – for now. Tomorrow I will go back to work to recover.

A week later I am on my way to Fenmere to start my part-time instructing job. I did my night shifts at work; I have had my sleep day. So now it's two days away and then one more day at home before the next work cycle. This new routine will take some getting used to, but compared to some of the things I have had to do in the past, this is nothing!

True to form the weather is awful. It is absolutely pouring down and blowing a gale as I drive into the car park. At least this time I didn't send any gravel flying when I turned into the entrance.

I make my way to the clubhouse and am greeted by a lady behind reception.

'You must be the new instructor,' she seems very friendly, 'picked a right day to start work, haven't you? How about you settle in with a cup of tea and I will go and get my son.'

'I see you have met my mum, Jean?' Leo joins me in the kitchen. 'She is effectively the office manager. I don't know what I would do without her. We are very much a family business, you see. You'll soon meet my Dad, John, who is the company accountant.'

Well, that's got to be a good thing. That means they are bound to work together really well. There is a lot to be said for a good team atmosphere.

Leo and I finish our teas and he shows me around the building. I am quite impressed with the little school.

Reception doubles as a little shop, where all sorts of aviation memorabilia are for sale, as well as lots of flying books, and anything and everything that the students require for their licence training. There are a few comfortable chairs scattered around a coffee table, which is covered in flying magazines.

Behind the table a door leads into a tiny kitchen, where, Leo assures me, sandwiches are made and provided free to all working staff. This is a most unusual and most welcome arrangement I must say.

Another door leads into a hallway, which in turn leads to two class rooms. The hall way itself has got a huge table in it, for flight planning, as well as two computers, so students and instructors can gain access to the latest weather.

The place is not unlike Adam's field. I feel at home already.

By lunch time, the weather has got worse, and most of the flying students have cancelled for the day, bar a few who are coming in for a chat.

We all have lunch in the restaurant and, having established that the weather is not going to change, Leo decides to call it a day.

'No point hanging on if it's like this, he says. Why don't you let me show you Aileen's B&B? You might as well settle in, and then come back first thing in the morning, when we can hopefully do some work.'

Oh well, it looks like an afternoon off for me.

I follow Leo in the car, three miles south, along the country lanes, then left at the cross roads and right at the windmill, only to find ourselves in an even smaller lane, where Leo pulls up in front of a large stone house.

He rings the doorbell. A woman about my age opens the door, but before she can introduce herself, a golden retriever squeezes past her and bolts out of the front gate, the woman in hot pursuit. A couple of minutes later they are back.

'This is Sid,.' she introduces the dog. 'We haven't had him long and he keeps escaping...oh, I'm Aileen by the way.'

Sid looks at me with big brown eyes and I have forgotten in an instant that I am actually quite nervous about dogs! We are going to be just fine.

Leo and I follow Aileen into the kitchen, which is huge and reminds me of Alison's and Jo's house back in Bournemouth, with its big kitchen table in the middle.

After a cup of tea and a chat, Leo is on his way home and Aileen shows me up to my room. My God! It's like the Hilton!

I am greeted by a cosy bed with a thick duvet, the bed spread matching the curtains, country style furniture, a digital radio and TV and an en-suite bathroom with a power shower and heated towel rail. I am amazed! I don't think this should be called a B&B; it's more like a five star hotel. It is absolutely fantastic!

The room rate is very reasonable, too, but catering is my own affair. I am allocated a kitchen cupboard, just like I was in Bournemouth.

'There is a little shop around the corner that stocks most things,' advises Aileen, 'or a supermarket five miles down the road.'

As it is still early, I decide to drive to the supermarket to get a few basics and something to eat for tonight. On my return I find Aileen in the kitchen preparing dinner, with Sid by her side, who is eyeballing the food as if his life depended on it.

'Sometimes we just have to ban him from the kitchen,' she sighs. 'He seems to be absolutely obsessed with eating anything in sight. He even licks the plates in the dishwasher. You could be forgiven for thinking we do not feed him at all.'

Sid looks guiltily at the floor for a moment, then watches me with renewed interest as I pack away my shopping. I shall have to be sensible and not feed him, I decide, but I can see he will be difficult to resist.

I go upstairs to change, and when I come down again Aileen's husband, Sam, has arrived home from work.

'Oh hello, you must be the new arrival,' he greets me with a grin, before giving Aileen a hug.

'Sam is a flying instructor at a nearby military school,' explains Aileen, 'so you are bound to have lots to talk about.'

We have indeed. The two of them are good company and the evening goes by in a flash. I will try and have an early night as tomorrow could be a very busy day, at least if the weather improves.

By Saturday morning the grey clouds have lifted and the wind has died down. As a result it is very misty, but hopefully things are going to improve later on. At half past eight I leave the B&B and make my way back to Fenmere.

'Fantastic B&B,' I say to Leo as he walks in.

'Didn't think you'd be disappointed,' he returns, 'It is rather a special place, and not many people know about it. They also take people long term, you know. So if you are still looking for a room in July, it's worth mentioning it to Aileen.'

That would be brilliant. Well, things seem to really be falling into place for me here!

At eleven the mist is slowly beginning to lift, and it's good enough for Leo and I to go up to do my initial flight check. We have half an hour in the air over Spalding, before returning to the field for a few circuits. Leo is happy and signs me off.

'No more students this morning,' he says, 'but a few trial lessons this afternoon. We have given you a couple of those to start you off.'

By the afternoon the skies are a hazy blue and I am really looking forward to getting airborne properly. The club have three Cessna 150's and two Cessna 172's, which are four seaters. My two lessons today will be in the smaller aircraft. I decide to not plan a particular route and to see what the students want to do.

It turns out they are not too fussed either, so I treat the two lessons as a 'getting to know the area exercise'. Both students are quite happy taking control as soon as we are in level flight, and I have a good look at the whole area, in order to get my bearings.

Leo's advice was to navigate by dykes and power stations, and that turns out to work incredibly well indeed. I touch down again at Fenmere, and have a similar flight with lesson number two. Before I know it, my first two days are over.

As I'm driving home to Stansted that night I'm on a high! I might not have flown as much as I had planned, but nonetheless I decide to call it a success. I'm on to a good thing here, I just know it. The stress and tension of the last few weeks is beginning to ease off.

Over the next few weeks I settle into a comfortable pattern. Six days at work, followed by day-off number one at home to recover and do my chores. Off to Fenmere early on day two, in time for my nine o'clock start. The drive is easy before the rush hour, and usually leaves me time to munch my sandwiches before I get out of the car. Home again on day three, leaving a proper day off on day four, where I can do as I please. House sale paperwork as well as further job hunting is taken care of during my work cycle.

Okay, this schedule doesn't leave much room for manoeuvre and I must admit, I wouldn't like to do it for a long period, but bearing in mind that I will be a full time flyer in July, I can put up with it.

The episode with a lot of upheaval

Packing boxes is always chaos, but to pack things up, not knowing when and where I am going to unpack them again feels particularly strange. Where will I be? Will I stay in the London area, or will I find a job up North, Manchester maybe or even Glasgow? Who knows! Just now I mustn't be sentimental. I have to be practical.

It is the beginning of June and my house move is just two weeks away. My plans to move at the end of June were thwarted by a very insistent Mrs Winton who was determined to complete by the end of May. In the end we compromised.

I will be moving in with Brian for two weeks, before making my way up to Aileen's B&B, where I did indeed manage to secure a permanent room for a very reasonable weekly rent. Aileen and Sam were happy to have me, and I could not think of a place where I would rather stay.

I have managed to get rid of most of my furniture, and my friend Steve has organised a van to transport the rest across to Brian's place. Everything is planned in minute detail. It's just a question of actually making it happen.

I continue with my normal routine as I am waiting for moving day to arrive. As the mail drops on the doorstep, I remind myself that I must pop to the post office in order to redirect everything to Brian's house. I absentmindedly pick up the mail and drop it on the kitchen table. An envelope catches my eye. I am not too excited as I open it. It is probably another rejection letter.

'... and we would be delighted if you could make yourself available for an interview.' I read the words over and over again. I cannot believe it. I can't even remember applying to Global Bizjets, a small executive outfit based at London City Airport. What do they fly? Golfstreams – how fantastic!

I look at the letter again. As luck would have it, the interview is on June 6th, which is actually a day off. Oh gosh, that leaves me just four days to prepare! I will just have to give it my best shot! I immediately telephone the number on the letter to confirm that I will be attending.

Then I hit the internet, which unfortunately does not give a lot away. I dive into my 'basic aviation knowledge cards' and refresh my brain on anything they might ask me on the technical side. At nine p.m. I stop as I will have to go to work. Well, at least it's a night shift, so plenty of time to read stuff. I have so got to nail this!

On the morning of June 6th I am making my way to London City Airport, dressed immaculately in my interview suit, and feeling reasonably confident.

There are eight of us in the group, for three positions, so we are told. The day begins with a technical quiz, the content of which was very much covered by the aviation knowledge cards. No surprises here, so far, so good.

In the afternoon we are called before the panel, one by one. The emphasis seems to be very much on enthusiasm and dedication to the job, which is pretty much my strong point. I answer the questions and throw in the odd question myself. It's going well, I just know it.

As I drive home again along the M25, I have this really good feeling! I know it all seems too good to be true at the moment, but I might just have been successful here. They have promised to let us know within a fortnight. So I might as well forget about it for now.

The next fortnight is so busy, that I can hardly think about the interview. There are a few last minute boxes to pack, and removal things to organise, plus there is work of course and I will be off to Fenmere for the usual two days in the middle of my days off.

Before I know it it's moving day! As good as his word, Steve turns up in his van and we start loading furniture. We will have to make two trips to transport this lot: The first load is going to his sister's house. Jane has just got divorced, is starting out on her own, and has bought most of my furniture.

On the second trip we will take the rest of my furniture over to Brian's. We have got to be done by twelve.

Two hours later the first trip has been completed, and I am about to pack up my computer, which would be the last item to go with load two.

'Might as well just check my e-mail before I switch it off.' I say to Steve, who nods in agreement as he is busy shifting my kitchen table.

'Steeeeve!'

He almost drops the table but manages to put it down before joining me in the lounge. I just want him to see what I am seeing, or otherwise I am not going to believe it. There, black on white, are the very words that I have been waiting for:

'... and we are pleased to offer you employment as a First Officer Global Bizjets, commencing 1st October, 2006. The written confirmation will be in the post to you shortly.'

Steve looks as shell-shocked as I am. 'Well-done mate,' he says at last. 'We'll have a beer in the pub later.'

I spend the rest of the day in a daze. I cannot believe I have actually got a flying job. And October is brilliant! I will still spend the summer flying instructing, so I won't have to let Leo down.

With great difficulty I put the good news to the back of my mind and carry on with the house move.

By nine o'clock that evening Steve, Brian and I are in the curry house having a little celebration, with all my furniture stored in one spare room, and myself settled in the other, just for the next fortnight.

'I think you should be a bit cautious and not really celebrate too hard, until you have received your letter of confirmation,' remarks Brian cautiously.

He is always sooo pessimistic, puts a damper on everything!

'On the other hand, you have already resigned, so it won't really make a difference whether you wanted to celebrate or not,' he adds cautiously as he sees my exasperated face.

We enjoy our curry and drink to my success. To be honest I was really dreading today, it was such a massive step. Then the day has turned out so much better than expected. If nothing else, I'll drink to that.

During the next fortnight Brian and I share lifts to work, since we both work the same shifts at Stansted and now both live under the same roof, albeit in name only.

I am beginning to feel all unsettled again, as my last day at work arrives, but then I remind myself that I do not have to worry as I have a job to go to now!

That said – my letter has still not arrived. Well, I won't be starting until October, so there probably is no mad rush. They probably have a million and one things to do in their office, with writing joining letters the last on the priority list. Still, I am keen to know more. Where will I be based? Where will the course be? Should I be finding somewhere to live? I am just so excited, I want to know all the details, so it will all seem more real!

With everyday that passes, my feeling of unease grows. When it has grown to a level way beyond my comfort zone, I decide to contact Tony, one of the other two candidates with whom I had thankfully swapped phone numbers. It turns out that he has not had his letter, either. I am probably just paranoid!

Meanwhile in the world of air traffic Brian and I turn up for what is to be my penultimate afternoon shift. We popped into the supermarket on the way to pick up a box of doughnuts. Brian's attitude is to buy the doughnuts first and then think of an excuse afterwards. It works for me!

In my first break in the tower, I scoff my doughnut and leaf through the airport paper. I do a double take on the headline. '*Local operator to acquire Global Bizjets*'. Some sort of take-over? Is that what the problem is? I must find out immediately what's going on!

I spend every break trying to get hold of Global Bizjets, all to no avail. I am constantly in the holding queue, and on one occasion, when I finally do get through nobody seems to know anything. I shall just have to wait and see what it says in my letter, when and *if* it finally arrives. I speak to Tony again, and he is very pessimistic.

'Don't think there'll be a job at all now, you know. They will probably have some sort of consolidation period.'

Damn! He's probably right. Good job I haven't told many people. I will just have to go back to plan A. After all, that was what I had planned in the first place. The trouble is, in the first place that plan had made me happy. Having made progress from there, it now seems like a poor consolation prize.

Bearing in mind yesterday's shocking news, my last day at Stansted is not a happy one! It would have never been easy at the best of times leaving a place of work where I have been happy for fifteen years, but throw in the additional disappointment about the job that never was and I get that familiar sick feeling in my stomach again. Still, I had that feeling when I sold my house, and look how well that turned out!

I have almost a week to go until I start my full time job at Fenmere. My friend Maria, who is half Maltese, has invited me to spend three days in Malta. She has a flat down there, so it will be a cheap break, and I desperately need one!

We fly down to Malta on Tuesday morning and spend three days in the sun. Night time parties intermingle with daytime get-togethers, which are leaving me no time to ponder on my situation. On Friday I am back, refreshed, happy and with a new lease of life. Let the adventure continue!

The episode where everything is fun

It is Sunday morning and I am getting organised for my move to Fenmere. I am hoping that the sunny weather is a sign of things to come. I mean I could really do with a good summer here, since I will be spending most of it in the air.

My room at the B&B will be small but cosy, with its usual five star standard including the fabulous bathroom. The rent is very reasonable and is inclusive of bills and laundry service – it doesn't get much better than that!

Yet again I am packing everything my little car will hold: A reasonable amount of clothes including my blue and white uniform for the flying school, my computer, some stationery, a clothes horse (I know the clothes horse was probably over the top but it will probably save on ironing), a linen basket and of course my flight bag. As an afterthought I throw in my iron, my favourite mug and a treat for Sid. I am so glad I won't need to worry about bedding and towels!

Everything else gets boxed up and joins my furniture in Brian's spare room. That's it. I'm done. I'm on my way to Fenmere.

As I pull onto the gravel drive, Sid comes bouncing out to greet me. He runs around in circles, keeps jumping up at me and finally sits down giving me his cute look.

'Ok Sid, just don't think this is going to be a sign of things to come,' I tell him with emphasis as I give him his treat. I am not entirely sure he's catching my drift though.

There is a lot of activity in the garden, as everybody is making the best of the summer weather. Aileen and Sam are playing table tennis. Mike and Janice, who live in the rented flat attached to the house, are in the Jacuzzi. Some other people who turn out to be holiday makers are playing volleyball.

'Barbecue tonight,' Sam has spotted me and interrupts his game to say hello.

'Sounds fantastic,' I grin, making a mental note to pick up some wine from the supermarket.

'You are happy where you are going, aren't you?' Aileen, bright red in the face from her table tennis efforts, is joining us.

'No problem,' I retort.

I quickly unpack the car, so I can join into the fun outside. Sid is more of a hindrance than a help, as he is sniffing every single item that leaves the boot of my car, in case it's edible.

'Don't worry about the dog,' reassures Sam. 'He knows he is not allowed upstairs.'

The baby gate on the stairs has made me wonder…so that's what it's for!

It takes me about an hour to unpack the car. I am not too worried where I will put everything at this stage. I am not working until Tuesday, so I will have plenty of time to sort everything out tomorrow.

I shut the door and make my way to the supermarket. There I get the usual bits and pieces and a small crate of white wine for the barbecue. I add two bags of marshmallows and a pack of skewers and make my way to the till.

As I get back to the B&B, more guests have arrived and the party is in full swing! Luckily the dress code is 'anything goes', so I will fit right in. I pop upstairs and get changed into my shorts and T-shirt. I love parties and meeting new people and all that social stuff!

It's turning out to be a fantastic evening! We spend another couple of hours playing games and cooling off in the Jacuzzi, whilst Sam and Mike are claiming sole ownership of the barbecue. Mike is a professional chef and loves nothing more then improvising with food, whilst Sam is a willing assistant, keen to pick up a few tips.

Finally the food is ready and it was well worth waiting for! We have salmon with rosemary and garlic, home made chicken satays, and superb spare ribs. Meanwhile Aileen has produced jacket potatoes and an array of salads, and Janice returns from her flat carrying garlic bread to be added to the already stupendous spread. We wash it all down with litres of wine and I must admit I am feeling quite tiddly.

Once all the food is cleared away and made Sid-safe, we come to the highlight of the evening. Aileen and Sam know how to do things in style.

We are sitting on the patio, marshmallows and skewers at the ready and have formed a neat row facing the stable wall, which is now used as a cinema screen. Sam is fiddling in the background, and suddenly the stable wall comes to life with small film classics in black and white.

All the while, the barbecue has died down to toasting level, and Aileen and Janice are taking it in turns to supply everyone with hot marshmallows for pudding.

It is an evening to remember. We are having so much fun – time is flying by. As the first people are leaving, I am surprised to see that it is past three a.m. and we can see the first rays of sun light in the east. I help with the clearing up and manage to be in bed by four. My room still looks like a bomb has hit it. I will have to tidy up in the morning, well, much later in the morning anyway.

There is plenty of time to tidy up on Monday as the day starts grey and drizzly. At about six a.m. this morning I was woken up by the most massive thunderstorm. It was not surprising really bearing in mind how sticky it had been in the evening. I tried to hide under the pillow in order to block out the noise. That must have been quite successful as it is now eleven o'clock.

I pop downstairs and have some breakfast. Everyone else seems to be out, including Sid, so I get to eat in peace.

Afterwards I pop upstairs again to finally sort out my room. When I have finished everything looks really cosy and feels like home already.

The grey mistiness outside has begun to lift promising another day of sunshine. I am pleased it is dry today, as every Monday the flying school is closed and maintenance is carried out, such as the mowing of the runway. The runway at Fenmere is so short, that the length of the grass makes a critical difference to the field length required for take-off. They mow it on a Monday, weather permitting. Aircraft performance is therefore best on a Tuesday, which makes for a good start of the working week. It will then slowly deteriorate until the next mowing a week later. So a rainy Monday can really spoil your week entirely!

Now I am organised, I decide to spend the rest of the day getting to know my immediate surroundings. I grab a bottle of water and my walking boots, and I'm off. Best not tell Sid about this – he'd be jealous!

On Tuesday morning it is still sunny as I make my way to the flying school. Now I am full-time, I start my days at ten o'clock and finish between six and eight in the evening, depending on my bookings.

'Morning,' Jean greets me with a smile, 'very busy day ahead.' She hands me the schedule. 'Oh, and before I forget, would you like salad sandwiches for lunch?'

It is so nice to not have to worry about bringing my own food! I'll eat anything I'm given, with the exception of animal organs and small children.

'That would be lovely,' I reply, and look at the plan to see how my day will pan out.

My first student is a new chap, who, having had his trial lesson, decided that he simply had to learn to fly! Today will be his turn to just go and fly in a straight line and at the same level. That should be an easy start for me, if not for him.

My second lesson is not a lesson as such, just a flight with a chap who holds a licence already but who has not flown for a while and would like an instructor next to him, as a safety net. We go off and look at the country side. I get him to fly a few manoeuvres and then throw in a few surprises, which he handles well. I want him to feel confident when he goes home tonight.

It's as busy as I have ever seen it! I am struggling to stay on schedule, as I fly, refuel and do my briefings with the students, scoffing bits of sandwich in between.

I do two trial lessons in the afternoon, before another thunderstorm stops play.

'It gets easier once you send people solo,' says Leo, having watched me juggling all my responsibilities today, 'but well-done for staying on schedule despite your workload. Not many people manage that.'

It's nice to have a compliment on my first full-time day at work. I come home exhausted but happy.

Wednesday is my other day off. So I get to work Tuesdays, then Thursdays till Sundays. It's quite nice having two days off, with one day of work in the middle. It's almost like having three days off in a row.

It's another sunny day and I decide to spend it on the river boat, and looking around Spalding. I do love this area. I could live here permanently, no problem.

On Thursday morning the flying continues and the weather shows no sign of getting any worse. Bar the odd thunderstorm in the afternoon, every day is perfectly flyable.

The week rushes by and I get to know new students as well as flying with the regulars. Before I know it, it's another weekend.

'This is someone you might want to have a look at,' says Leo handing me Les's file. 'I think this needs a different approach.'

It is Sunday morning and Les is a Sunday regular. At 85 years old, he is not your average student. According to his file he started having lessons about a year ago, and, whereas he always gets quite good towards the end of a lesson, he will have forgotten all of it by the beginning of the next. As I walk into the clubhouse, Les is already waiting for me.

'Hello Les, shall we go flying?' I greet him.

'Pardon?'

'Shall we go up and see how we get on?'

'I'm sorry Dear, I can't hear you, hearing aid's playing up again. If you give me one of those paper clips, I can sort it out.'

I pass him a paper clip and Les fiddles with his hearing aid. This is going to be good!

The procedure improves his hearing only marginally, but just enough to convince him to get into the aeroplane, and off we go.

Immediately after take-off he is overtaken by events. I take control and point us in the right direction again, having turned his headset up to full volume, so he can make out what I am saying. Sadly though, that does not seem to improve his flying much. I keep needing to take control and decide to go back to basics, but even that proves too much for him.

The entire lesson is a succession of mishaps and reminds me a little too much of the training flights I did with Celia on my instructor's course. However, true to form and with minutes to go, Les seems to suddenly get the hang of it, and we manage to fly in a straight line for the first time since we took off.

The point is though that the whole time, even in his worst moments in the air, Les is having fun. He is having a great time all the way through, and I haven't got the heart to spoil his day.

I say as much to Leo later.' As long as he realises he is never going to go solo, what is the harm in him continuing with his lessons?' I suggest.

'We are going to need to tell him he will never gain his licence,' adds Leo with a frown. 'Then he has the full picture and can make his own decision on whether to carry on or not.'

'And if he does decide to carry on, at least there is no pressure to carry on with a particular syllabus,' I add, 'we could just focus on the fun of it. He's a lovely chap, bit of a character. I'll fly with him.'

'Are you sure?' Jean looks up from her paper work.

'Absolutely,' I grin, 'I like a bit of variety, and it can safely be said that Les is an important component in the variety stakes.'

That decision made, they tell Les the news, and he is more than happy to come flying every Sunday, with me as his dedicated instructor.

A couple of weeks later he requests to change to the four seater, as 'it is easier to get in and out of.'

'Why not?' I agree happily, 'the four seater it is, Les. See you next week.'

The weather is still dry and sunny a week later, and as I get to the flying school, Les is waiting for me already, with a lady in tow.

'Edith is my neighbour,' he introduces her cheerfully, 'don't suppose we could take her up with us could we, now we have some seats in the back. It's just I promised to take her flying.'

'I don't see why not,' I agree as we walk over to the aeroplane. I get Edith settled in the back and make her familiar with the safety instructions, and off we go.

No pressure for Les today, just a bit of fun flying the aeroplane around the houses, including his own, and that of his lady friend. Edith is very impressed with his flying skills and Les' grin seems to be wider than normal.

The Sunday after that Les introduces me to Bertha. 'Oh, Les is ever so clever,' says Bertha in awe, as we land again.

Les seems to have reached celebrity status in his neighbourhood, as he turns up with a different lady every weekend. All of them are admiring his flying skills, and far be it from me to put them in the picture. He is a bit of a lad, I must say, not entirely without admiration.

The whole summer Les is having fun, until one day in September, he fails to turn up for his lesson. Later that month we find out that he has passed away. No doubt he died a happy man!

When I made the decision to work here full time, I would have never guessed how well this would turn out and how much fun I was going to have! I get into a comfortable routine of flying days and my two days off a week, which are usually spent sightseeing. I have not got two pennies to rub together, but that doesn't greatly bother me – for now.

Also I am incredibly lucky with the weather! The summer of 2006 has been a scorcher; I cannot remember another one like it.

Meanwhile the job hunting continues, with the usual lack of success. I am getting so used to rejections that my expectations have dropped to a level where disappointment is impossible. Then one day I decide to write this really silly letter, more to let out my frustrations than anything else:

Dear Sirs,

Like so many other letters you will have received today, this is yet another job application. Like so many other people I have passed all my exams first time, got good results and am now supposed to convince you that I am the pilot you are looking for.

Far be it from me to pretend that you are the only airline for me, as you know as well as I do that I have applied to

everybody else anyway. What I can say, however, is that if you do decide to take me on, then I will be the best I can be (which is usually quite good).

On the strength side, I am an enthusiastic and willing participant in any training given and am flexible on location, since my property as well as any domestic commitments have long since fallen victim to my flying career, such as we know it.

My weaknesses are singing, embroidery and childcare, which are thankfully not required in aviation.

I am a part-time self-improver who has never been to Oxford, is no longer a spring chicken and is currently flying Cessna's for a living.

As such I have nothing else to offer but unlimited enthusiasm and commitment to my chosen career. If that is enough, then I would be delighted to hear from you,

Kind regards, …

At first I just write the letter. Then I think, why not post it to few airlines – what the hell! Things can't get any worse. Whilst it makes me feel better, I have no expectations whatsoever.

So it comes as a great surprise, when a week later, I find I have another invitation for an interview.

The episode with a lot of promise

'... and we look forward to seeing you on Monday 15th August at 9a.m.' the letter finishes.

Okay, I think coolly, no point getting too excited this time. Since the fiasco with Global Bizjets I have experienced a number of time wasters. There was the airline who invited me along just to 'make up the numbers' to then take on only their ex-cabin crew, and the airline that had made me pay to be interviewed only to tell me on the day that I wasn't in the age bracket they were looking for. Last but not least there was the foreign outfit that kept putting off simulator dates and eventually disappeared from the radar altogether. So, excuse me if I don't hyperventilate with excitement just because I have an interview with Scottish Worldwide.

Still - I must prepare myself and give it my best shot. I decide to take the Sunday before off work in order to make my way up to Edinburgh. Leo is quite happy to lose me for one day.

'Good Luck,' he says and I know he means it, 'Although it would be a shame to lose you'.

There is a local flight from East Midlands at 4 p.m. As I am constantly accused of being over organised, I decide to try the relaxed approach this time. I will find a hotel when I get there. I have the whole afternoon to do it in. How difficult can it be?

As I get to the airport however, I realise that my plan might be a little flawed. The departure board shows a two hour delay as the airport has been hit by thunderstorms all afternoon. That delay turns out to be three hours by the time we are actually on our way.

At Edinburgh things are no better and we are held for thirty minutes before they allow us to land. By the time I am finally in the arrival hall, it is 9p.m.

I make my way over to the hotel desk.

'You would have to be extremely lucky to find any accommodation in Edinburgh tonight' are the words I am greeted with. 'The summer is always busy and what with the festival…'

Oh no! The festival! How could I forget? So much for trying *not* to be organised! Well, I have managed it, and now I will be sleeping on an airport bench, by the looks of things.

I wait patiently as the hotel agent makes phone call after phone call. Twenty minutes later I have a room, at the opposite end of town to where I want to be. She quotes a three figure sum, and that does not even include breakfast. It does cross my mind that I am being ripped off here, but I am in no position to argue. I take the room and go outside to hail a cab.

The journey takes a good forty minutes. The Scottish Worldwide building is at the airport and I decide to allow an hour for the same journey in the morning. This is all going to cost a fortune by my current standards. I hope it will be worth it!

At a quarter to nine the next morning I knock on the door of Scottish Worldwide. The door is answered by a very smart looking office girl, who is showing me to the waiting area. I am the first candidate to be interviewed. Now I am nervous, whether I like it or not.

Fifteen minutes later I am still waiting, when a man from the office sits down next to me and starts what appears to be general chit chat. I cannot help the feeling that I am being interviewed already and chose my answers carefully. I then turn the game around and ask him a few things. My internet research has not been terribly successful, and this is my one and only chance to get a bit of information, before I go in any time soon.

The man is surprisingly easy to talk to and is only too happy to tell me about the company, its history and its future plans. My brain is like a sponge. I must try and remember as many important facts as I can here.

'Oh well, best get on,' says the man eventually and makes his way back to his office. I am left alone again, and five minutes later I am called before the interview panel.

As I enter the room I cannot believe my eyes! The man I have just been chatting to is actually part of the panel. He begins to ask me questions.

'So, you would like to fly for Scottish Worldwide, What can you tell me about the company?' His face does not betray the fact that we have just been chatting.

What's this all about? We have just been talking. If I just repeat everything he has just told me, he will probably think that I'm a bull shitter. However, if I don't, he might think that I am exceptionally stupid, and then I would have lost altogether!

I decide to go with the optimistic view. He was probably just being helpful. So I repeat all the facts that I found out less than ten minutes ago, albeit in my own words.

'You know a lot about the company!' the man nods approvingly.

I am trying hard not to look puzzled.

'Any more questions from you, Bill?' He turns to the man on his right, who is clearly one of the company's senior pilots.

The questions that follow are mainly technical and do not pose a great problem. Before I know it I am on my way back to the airport to catch my flight home.

That went well, definitely, no doubt in my mind. But I mustn't get too excited here or get my hopes up. It's best to just forget about it now until I hear one way or the other, which, so they told me, could be weeks away. By midday I have landed back at East Midlands and make my way home to the B&B.

On Tuesday morning I am back at work. I try really hard to put the whole interview thing to the back of my mind. That said I cannot help being a slave to my phone for the first few days, but by the weekend I am managing to let go a little. Flying instructing has resumed its normal pattern.

As summer turns into autumn, the weather is still good, but the thunderstorms are more frequent, and the wind has picked up.

As I wake up one Saturday morning, the curtains are billowing and the trees are bending in the wind. It is the middle of September and it looks like we have the first of the autumn gales.

I have to brush the leaves of my car before I can make my way to the flying school. The road is an obstacle course, as lots of fallen branches are littering the road. Good job there are no trees near the airfield.

As I get to Fenmere, Leo has already been up for a quick weather check.

'It's a bit rough up there,' he admits, 'but flyable for now, seeing as the wind is down the runway for once.'

I look at the book to see who my first students are. Not everyone is going to get benefit from going up in this sort of weather. I'm pleased to see I have two trial lessons. They can go, but I must warn them about the turbulence.

It turns out that the trial lessons are in fact a married couple, who are booked in to fly, one after the other. I lead them through to the classroom and proceed with my usual briefing.

'Now, I must be honest with you,' I finish, 'it is pretty turbulent up there today, which is by no means dangerous but could be slightly uncomfortable. I am more than happy to fly with you, but by the same token you are welcome to postpone things to another day.'

'Well we have had a long drive, so we are going up,' says the woman, who is clearly very determined.

'Brilliant,' my smile is genuine. 'Who would like to go first?'

I expected the woman to leap forward with enthusiasm, and am therefore surprised when it is the man, Ed, who puts himself forward, albeit somewhat reluctantly.

'Well, I might as well get it over with,' he says, clearly uncomfortable with the idea, but not wanting to look a coward in front of his wife.

'Ok let's go and have some fun,' I smile encouragingly, well aware that he is not altogether happy about going up in this weather.

As we walk out to the aeroplane I feel I should emphasize an important point.

'If ever you are uncomfortable when we are in the air, do not hesitate to tell me. We can come back early, and you can fly off the rest of your lesson on a calmer day, no problem. The idea is to enjoy yourself.'

Ed nods in reply and we are on our way. The wind is blowing twenty five knots down the strip and even the taxi out is interesting. I tuck a few sick bags under my kneeboard, so I can grab one quickly without them being on show. Once a student catches a glimpse of a sick bag he will use it. If I have learned nothing else about flying in rough weather, I have learned that.

'Still happy to go?' I glimpse at Ed who looks pale and is hanging on to his seatbelt like dear life.

He nods again. I hope words have not failed him at this early stage!

I quickly do my checks and make my way onto the runway and take off.

It's not so bad at first, but it soon becomes apparent that we are not in for a smooth ride. I level off and let Ed take the controls.

He is doing quite well for the first ten minutes. Then he gets uncomfortable.

'Not feeling well,' he squeezes out between deep breaths. 'Want to go back, you fly.'

I take control and turn the aeroplane around. Now we have the wind behind us, things go from rough to totally silly. The little Cessna is being battered by the gusts, and I am reminded of that fateful day when I first went up on my IR course, only this time it is not me who is feeling sick. Ed has gone from white to grey and I decide that now is the time to hand him a sick bag. To my surprise he waves it away.

'Want to go back!' He is now screaming at me.

'We will be back on the ground in less than ten minutes,' I reassure him as I steer the aircraft back towards Fenmere. I try and encourage him to put his hands on the controls with me, just to take his mind away from his airsickness, but Ed is having none of it!

'Want to go back, want to go back!' He is completely panicking now and nothing will calm him down. Meanwhile we are all over the place as I make my way sideways towards the field. I radio in to get the first aider to meet us at the aircraft, as I am quite seriously concerned that Ed might pass out.

I fly the shortest approach of my life and put the aeroplane down abeam the parking area.

'That's it, you are back' I say to Ed, who has gone from grey to green and just manages to nod.

The first aider is waiting for us at the gate, pleased that his skills are not required after all. He is joined by Ed's wife who is running out towards the aeroplane.

'Are you alright?' she asks Ed with what appears to be a voice of concern.

'Better now,' mumbles Ed, the colour slowly returning to his face.

'He just felt a little sick,' I remark, totally unprepared for the scene that was to follow.

'There is always something wrong with you,' shouts the wife, proceeding to hit him with her handbag. 'You bloody wimp! You are hopeless you are.' The blows keep coming.

We watch Ed running from the aeroplane, covering his head and making his way to the car park, all the while being pursued by his wife still hitting him. He bypasses the clubhouse and picks up speed but there is no getting away from her.

There is no point me trying to join the race to give Ed his well-earned trial lesson certificate. So instead I watch them run off into the distance towards their car, never to be seen again.

We get a lot of mileage out of the incident as we are having lunch in the clubhouse afterwards. Needless to say flying has stopped for the day.

There have been a few interesting incidents with sick trial lesson students over the summer, not all of them as funny as this one, and not all of them with such a clean outcome.

Leo went up on a very hot and hazy day in August, only to realise he had forgotten his stash of sick bags. He did not want to come back and was relying on luck, which turned out to be misplaced optimism. His student was extremely ill and covered every surface in the aeroplane, including Leo, from head to toe.

Since the day was busy and Leo did not want to lose precious flying time by going home to change, he took advantage of the summer weather and asked Jean to hose him down with the garden hose, in the clothes he stood up in. He was soon clean again although soaked to his skin, until he dried naturally as he kept working.

I myself was unlucky only a weak later, when one of our four seaters broke down, and we managed to borrow a private aircraft, for just the one day. The aircraft was immaculate and unlike our training aircraft, equipped with carpets and curtains. Of all the aircraft to be sick in this wasn't the ideal target but yes, you guessed it, that was the day when my student cast the sick bag aside and aimed at the upholstery instead.

I spend hours that evening trying to restore the aircraft to its former glory, using my bodyweight in carpet cleaner and air fresheners in the process.

Oh, how I laughed! (Well, the others did, anyway).

Most of the time of course things are running smoothly and I am still having a good time. Trial lessons mix with flying students, and new students mix with more experienced ones. I have even sent off my first 'first solo', a young lad called Oscar who has ambitions of flying in the military and will no doubt go a long way.

As September turns into October, I finally receive my reply from Scottish Worldwide. I cannot believe it! I have actually got the job, together with three others. Oh my God! I am going to fly a 737!!

Now, if foresight was as good as hindsight, which is allegedly 20/20, I would have not been quite so delighted. I would have realised that I was about to open the biggest can of worms ever touched by human hands. As it stands however, I am as happy as a pig in clover! I got that long awaited job at last!

The episode with the best of intentions

The job does not start until January, but I decide to stop work at the end of November. There are a lot of things to organise, which I will put every effort into, at risk of looking over organised to the point of being boring. Once I am on my type rating course, self-financed as they so often are, I don't want any distractions. I just want to have one thing on my mind and that's passing the course.

Leo is very supportive as I hand in my notice. 'We are sorry to see you go,' he says, 'but we knew it was coming. All of our instructors leave eventually, if only to earn a decent living.'

The end of November soon approaches and I am both relieved and sad as I finish on my last day at Fenmere. Leo has organised a good send off at the local Italian, and everyone I know is going to be there. I feel choked all evening and am completely off my food. Leaving Stansted was hard, but this is so much more difficult! I promise to stay in touch as we all say our good-byes at the end of the evening, and the very next morning I do the same at the B&B.

Car full to brim, I am on my way down South to spend a month at Brian's place in order to get *really* organised.

Accommodation is the first thing on my mind. A hotel is too expensive; a B&B is not flexible enough. Ideally I need a two-month-house share, or student accommodation of some sort.

A search on the internet draws my attention to what looks like the ideal solution:

'Need somewhere to stay short-term? Hotel too expensive? Renting not possible? We have the answer. Contact Debbie at "rooms R us". Mature students welcome!'

That's perfect. That was made for me, I think as I fill in the form. Debbie calls me back the very next day and explains the system.

Apparently they will send a choice of accommodation. I will take my pick and pay a deposit, upon which the address is released and arrangements are made for me to move in on my chosen date.

I am pleased that Debbie has contacted me so quickly. She is clearly reliable and as organised as I am.

The accommodation list looks promising, too. I choose a room in a country house, just three miles from Jetmiles, where I will do my course. It promises to be close to the shops, non-smoking and full of all mod cons. I am lucky to have found this place and send my deposit off straight away.

A week later I have heard nothing, but I am concerned. I mean, I only sent the money on Sunda, will probably take a few days for the cheque to clear.

When nearly two weeks have passed without any news, I decide to give Debbie a call. Maybe I am just being too organised again? I refrain from leaving any urgent or impatient messages. I do not want to appear rude or mistrusting. Good relations are so important. Debbie is bound to contact me in the next week or so.

As much as I try to remain relaxed about the issue, I cannot shake off this feeling of unease. What if I have been conned in some way?

Christmas is fast approaching and I have still not heard from Debbie. Surely I should have had some sort of confirmation by now. I call her again, but all I get is the answer phone. I keep trying until just before Christmas and then again in the week leading up to New Year, but all to no avail.

On January third I am really worried. I am supposed to be moving in tomorrow, and I have no idea where. I keep trying and trying until I finally manage to get hold of her at eleven p.m.

'Oh dear that,' hesitates Debbie, 'I'm afraid I was out of the country for a couple of weeks and I'm only just getting round to catching up. Today? Oh no, there won't be anything available for at least another week. Why don't I send you another accommodation list? You then pick a place and send me some money...'

I am speechless, but not for long. 'I expect my deposit back within a week', I inform her, give her my address, and then put the phone down.

Oh rats! Now what do I do?! Well, if nothing else, I will make my way down to Gatwick, immediately, and once there, I will just have to see what I can find, B&B or otherwise, and then I will start my course tomorrow and keep the disaster to the back of my mind. But I can't help feeling angry – I had a month to sort this out and did everything I could – I so do not deserve this!

I leave the M23 and drive into Harfield, I tiny village just minutes away from Jetmiles. If I am going to find accommodation, I am going to find it here.

I park in the market square and walk along the high street, hoping to find an estate agent that is open on a Sunday. I am in luck.

The door chime announces my arrival and gets the attention of Nigel, the office manager.

'How can I help you?' asks Nigel cheerfully as he points me to a chair.

I fill him in on the details and ask him whether he has ever heard of Debbie or 'rooms R us'. He has not. I doubt I will ever see my deposit again, but I can worry about that later. Just now, I have more pressing things on my mind.

'So, the big question is' I conclude, 'have you got anything at all that we could work with here?'

Nigel's' face settles in a deep frown. 'It is not normally what we deal with,' he admits, 'but there is possibly one option I could come up with.'

I look at him expectantly, but when he describes the accommodation he had in mind my heart sinks. Shared house, full of partying cabin crew, smokers welcome, and not in an area one could recommend. It is exactly the sort of place I have been trying to avoid. I thank Nigel for his efforts and promise to be in touch before he shuts his office at 4 p.m.

There has got to be something better than this! I drive over to the airport itself and look at the notice board. There are several people advertising for tenants. I write down the telephone numbers, grab a coffee and make myself comfortable at a table in the corner.

The first number I call is not a huge success. They found a tenant a week ago and have forgotten to take the sign down.

The second number is incoherent. I have no idea what language they have just addressed me in, but it wasn't remotely related to English.

Number three sounds quite promising, until they realise I will only stay for two months. No matter how hard I try, there is no convincing them to take me on short term.

Number four is more than twenty miles south of the airport, in an area known for its lively goings on and above average crime rate. I refuse politely and ring off.

Okay, B&B's next. There must be somewhere in the area. It's another two hours before I have to get back to Nigel's office. I will use every minute in a last ditch attempt to get this sorted.

Unfortunately though, it is no good. The harder I look the sooner it becomes apparent that, if I stay in a B&B, no matter how basic, I will put myself on to dangerous territory financially. I cannot afford to delve into my reserves this early in the game, so with great reluctance I drive back to Nigel's office and ask to look at the room.

Nigel is delighted. Ten minutes later I follow him in my car as we make our way through the narrow streets of Harfield, and towards Woodside House.

My first impression is a good one. The house is on the corner, between the through road and a cul-de-sac, right next to a little shop. It is quite a modern building, and the outside is clean and tidy.

We walk through the front door into a tiny hall, behind which is a kitchen leading into the lounge. The kitchen is not as clean as I would have liked it, and the lounge smells of smoke, but it could be worse.

'Your room has just been decorated,' throws in Nigel, guessing my thoughts, as he leads the way up the staircase.

I am pleased to see that the room, although basic, appears to be clean. It still smells of new paint and does look quite promising. A bed in between build in wardrobes is the only piece of furniture but the carpet is brand new and so are the curtains which frame a window that stretches almost the entire length of the wall.

'There is even an en suite,' Nigel points out proudly, sensing my renewed enthusiasm, but as we open the door we both stop in our tracks and look on in disbelief!

The bathroom has clearly not been included in the redecoration process. The shower tray is black with mould, and a headless shower hose is hanging of what must have been its rail once. The shower door does not close properly and one of the panels has been shattered. There is a hole in the wall where there must have been a towel rail before, and the toilet has no seat on it.

'I can't live in here', is the first thought that comes to mind, but then I realise that this is it! This is my one and only option, and it is five pm.

'I take it,' I say and Nigel's face lights up, 'but we are going to have to come to some sort of arrangement here,' I continue.

'I am happy to sort out this bathroom but that will have to be reflected in my rent.'

Nigel considers his options. 'Let me have a word with the landlord,' he says and walks outside clutching his mobile.

Two minutes later we have a deal. I have two months' living for six weeks rent, provided I sort out the bathroom. Decorating a house was the last thing I expected to be doing this week, but I am going to need some sort of exercise whilst I am on this course, so this might as well be it. I pay my two weeks rent for my first month, and Nigel is on his way.

The next evening I find myself at the local D.I.Y. store, looking for the necessary items. Eventually I leave with a shower hose, a toilet seat, buckets of cleaning stuff and the sturdiest pair of rubber gloves I can find.

Once back at the digs I get to work. As I am scrubbing away, I reflect on my first day at Jetmiles. After a brief introduction we were shown to a class room to start studying for the ground school subjects. There were four of us in the group and it was good to meet Phil, who will be my partner in the simulator next month.

In the break I re-iterated my accommodation story which caused a lot of laughs. Phil, who, as a captain from another airline, has been provided with a hotel room on full expenses, laughed the loudest. Oh well, one day that will be me!

My efforts are making quite a difference and the bathroom is beginning to look the part. The mould is gone, the shower rail is fixed and sporting the new shower hose with a head on it. There is not a lot I can do about the broken panel, but I tape it over to stop it getting any worse. The sink is shining and the toilet can now be sat on.

I down tools at midnight and fall into bed. Things can only get better!

Good job I 'decorated' on day one, as all evenings are now taken up with studying.

The canteen at Jetmiles is excellent, and I am pleased I don't have to venture into the kitchen to cook at night. It has got worse since I first saw it. I don't think anybody ever does any washing up, and the rubbish keeps piling up in the corner.

Other things are beginning to bother me, too. There are constant parties going on in the lounge, and the music is blaring all night, making it impossible to get any sleep. I hate to be a spoil sport and far be it from me to speak up at the first sign of trouble, but it's beginning to be an issue. My exams are coming up and I wish I could just get some rest at some stage!

The next morning I decide to address the issue, but am shouted down.

'Boring!' shouts Aaron who is a long-haul steward and insists he needs the parties to wind down.

'You should join in, then you won't notice,' suggests his boyfriend.

Ok, I am boring and I am poor and therefore I have to live here, and whilst I am living here I shall have to jolly well pass that type rating course, because if I don't I will have missed my one and only chance of getting a job, and that would make me even poorer and even more boring!!

But I say nothing of course. I sense that I am not going to get anywhere here; I just have to put up with it. I have already spoken to the landlord, who suggested that we were going to sort this out amongst ourselves – great!

The exams are at the end of this week and, having spent another night trying to study with earplugs in, I finally give up and fall into bed. At three a.m. the parties resume. The music is so loud, it makes the walls vibrate, and the smoke seeping into my bedroom from downstairs is not just from cigarettes alone.

I decide enough is enough. If I want to pass my course, then I am going to have to get out of here, hang the expense! I vow to start looking at the weekend.

The ground school exams are done by the end of the week and flying is going to start on Monday. That gives me three days to find somewhere decent to stay. I enlist the help of the school. Their accommodation list mainly covers surrounding hotels, but luckily for me the secretary knows of a B&B that is as she calls it 'by no means the Hilton' but nice enough for a few weeks.

I wouldn't necessarily agree with her on the first part of her statement as the place looks absolutely lovely. It is quite reasonable with it and would be perfect, if they weren't going to start major building work in the following week. My simulator flying will run on a shift pattern, so as far as noise is concerned, it would be from the fire into the frying pan.

I am at the end of my tether here! So the solution comes as a surprise: One of the secretaries in the school has a brother who runs a B&B in Harfield. He relies mainly on holiday makers staying the night before their flight, and business is slack in the winter. 'Let me speak to him,' she suggests, 'he might just give you a good rate.'

On Saturday I am moving out of the shared house and into the B&B. I have a room under the roof, which is more expensive than the shared house but now a necessity. There is even a washing machine I can use. I move all my stuff, then ring Nigel to tell him I have moved on.

'The landlord is not going to be very happy,' he says with concern. 'You signed a contract to stay for two months, remember, and now you are moving out early, he could make your life very difficult.'

'I have also signed a contract promising clean and tidy accommodation and people on cleaning rotas,' I counter, 'and that's clearly not happened either. I lived there for a month and I paid for a month. If he can't keep his tenants maybe he should do something about the state of the place.'

Nigel seems happy with this argument and I'm not going to worry about potential repercussions, I have more important things on my mind.

The very next day we are going to start our training in the simulator. The grapevine suggests that, out of the two instructors that have been allocated to our course, one is meant to be very nice whereas the other one has been the subject of many complaints, and is only covering the course due to a staff shortage.

Do I feel lucky? Well, I will have to be lucky some time...

The episode with a lot of bad luck

I am in my B&B getting ready for the simulator, when my mobile rings. It's my mother. Okay, I should not have answered it, I should have just gone out of the door and rung her back later, but I did answer it, and my day suddenly took a terrible turn.

My mother is in floods of tears. I cannot make out what she is saying at first. Eventually, some words come out between sobs.

'It's your friend from school,' she says choking her words, 'she died this morning.'

What?? How is that possible, I mean we were the same age, grew up together, went out dating together ....

'Well, apparently she was very ill,' my mother continues, 'but she didn't want anyone to know.'

How can she have been very ill? I mean, I only saw her a month ago, and she looked the same as always, and she behaved the same as always and we had a right laugh, I am just not getting it!

Now, in fairness to my mother, she does not have a clue about the project I am involved in here. She just thought I'd want to know and of course I do, and now I am too shocked for words and I have to put it all to the back of my mind and go and fly a simulator. Sod the course! I am going to ring and speak to her husband.

'Cancer,' he says. 'She had known for a while. She just wanted everything to be normal and she was always so happy to see you, you know.'

Oh my God! Now I am in floods of tears, and I should have left here ten minutes ago. I put the phone down and try to regain some composure. I need to go and fly now. I need to pull myself together. My friend would understand.

I reach Jetmiles at a quarter past seven, fifteen minutes late. I apologise as I enter the class room. Phil gives me a questioning glance. I shall explain myself later.

'Late on your first day,' scolds the instructor, 'typical woman, had all day to get ready! Doesn't show the best attitude, does it?'

Oh great – we have got the nasty one of the bunch! (And I have just managed to piss him off!!)

I try to concentrate in the simulator but nothing I do is good enough. I spend two hours getting shouted at, and during the session my performance deteriorates even more.

The next evening is no better and my confidence hits rock bottom. This chap has really taken a dislike to me and I seem to be in a no win situation. If I could ever fly before, I seem to have lost my ability entirely. The harder I try the worse I get, and the worse I get the more stupid I feel, and the more stupid I feel the worse I get! It's a downward spiral!

'Get out of your seat!' barks the instructor and makes me sit in the back, 'you are not fit to be on this course!' The words cut like a knife, as I vacate my seat and take my place on the observer's bench.

Well, this is really going to help me, isn't it? I watch, as first the instructor does some flying, and then Phil has a go, all the while doing it beautifully.

'I want to see some improvement from you tomorrow,' barks Mr Angry, 'otherwise I'm going to recommend you get thrown off the course.'

Oh fab! Money well spent then! I could be out on my ear tomorrow, but I am not out on my ear just yet! It ain't over till it's over. I know I *can* do this!

That said, I have no idea how to improve anything tomorrow. Every time I so much as touch the controls, the instructor seems to lose his temper. I will just have to do my best and take it from there. But just the thought of it stresses me out. I feel worse every day. What on earth have I let myself in for?!!

The next evening I give things a go, and at the end of the session I still have a job.

'That was a bit better, now keep up the hard work, and don't you dare be late again!'

Phil thinks I am being victimised and advises me to take some action. I promise to give it some thought, but am reluctant. They have nobody else to replace this chap, and if I complain it might make him even angrier. I am also not too keen to admit to a personality clash this early in the game. I can't see the airline being too pleased about that. I decide to leave things as they are for now, and to use my days off to relax and refocus.

The days off do not start well, as my mobile rings at nine o'clock the next morning. It's the landlord of Woodside House, spitting feathers.

'You owe me a month's rent,' is his opening gambit.

'I don't believe I do,' is my reply. I have a feeling that this is not going to be an easy conversation.

Indeed it isn't. The landlord is irate, and I have had just about as much as I can take this week! I struggle to remain polite as I explain to him exactly why I was forced to move out, but my reasoning does not wash with him. No matter what I say, he insists that I owe him the money, and when I am still not convinced, he threatens to take me to court.

Oh great! Can this week get any better?

I spend the afternoon at the citizens' advice bureau in order to see what can be done. They advise me to offer the landlord a small sum as a good will gesture, as once accepted he apparently cannot sue me. So I'm effectively paying a bribe here – I am buying piece of mind. This whole venture is getting far more expensive than I bargained for! I have never spent so much money and had so little fun!

Ok, let's not panic – lets simply focus on the problem areas in my life and find solutions... number one: despite best efforts have accommodation issues with legal implications; number two: despite best efforts am crap on course; number three: despite best efforts spent far more money than anticipated. My life's a disaster! Lets just move on...

Two days later I am back in the simulator and subjected to the usual shouting. I have a cunning new strategy. I am going to ignore it. Things seem to go well until, on day five, they finally come to a head:

We have almost come to the end of the session when Mr Angry demands that I turn around to look at the panel behind me. It is not an unreasonable request, and I proceed to slowly turn around in my seat, bearing in mind the effect sudden movements can have on my back, especially when under stress. The last thing I need now is another back trouble episode ... that would probably be a career ending move!

The instructor is not happy. 'When I say turn around just bloody do it, don't sit there dithering and daydreaming!' He grabs my right arm and pulls it hard.

'Stop,' I scream knowing what is likely to happen next.

'What's the problem now? he screams back, his face white with fury. 'You can't even twist around properly? I bet you are crap in bed as well!'

The silence is deafening! I notice Phil glancing across at me wondering what I am going to do next, and I remember glancing across at Phil wondering whether he was on my side on this one.

'This session stops right here,' I say eventually. 'Stop the simulator!' I grab my things and walk out. That's it. I've had a gutful; I am going to have to do something now!

The very next morning I go and see the managing director of Jetmiles. He is polite and professional and listens to my description of events. Phil is there with me to confirm what has happened.

'Unfortunately I am unable to change your instructor just now,' says the managing director 'but I will have a word with him, and I can assure you that his behaviour will improve from now on.'

I am not entirely at ease with this turn of events, but I know when I am out of options. If I am not careful, I will be labelled as 'trouble', and I cannot afford that, whether I am at fault here or not.

Indeed, Mr Angry seems to have mellowed somewhat as we continue with our lessons. He is never going to be

Mr Nice guy, but the constant insults have stopped and the shouting has tuned down to a lower volume. Still, I am very reluctant to ask any questions and am just keen to get the sessions over with, with as little fuss as possible.

Later on I would find out to my detriment that this attitude was a mistake, and that I would find myself with knowledge gaps that would take months to iron out. Just for now however, this is the only way I can cope with the training!

Meanwhile Phil and I have become a good team and are doing our best to succeed. Two weeks later we pass the mock test, and that alone is a huge relief!

On the same day the other two in our group pass their final test first time. Now the pressure is on for us to do the same.

In the build up to the flight test I experience the worst case of nerves ever! I am not normally this bad, but I think the accumulation of events is finally taking its toll. My confidence has had a bad knock and I cannot help wondering what disaster is going to happen next.

I should be happy and relaxed as I have managed to solve most of my problems. I have even managed to track down Debbie from 'rooms R us', entirely by chance, through an advert I spotted at the airport. Having found out were her offices are, I summoned all my courage and paid her a visit demanding my deposit back.

It turned out that she never set out to deceive me – she is just terribly disorganised. When I introduced myself she was very apologetic and paid my money back straightaway, cash in hand no less! I suppose it did help to have my friend Dale standing next to me, who happens to be six foot five.

Good old Dale! He has been a pillar of support in the last few weeks. He came over twice to take me out for dinner and to practice all my flying stuff with me. As an Airbus pilot, he made a lot of Boeing jokes at my expense. It was like a breath of fresh air having him around!

Finally the big test day arrives, or at least day one of two. Phil and I are sitting in the foyer, sipping tea and waiting for the examiner to arrive.

I have no idea who the examiner is, but however bad he might be, he has got to be better than Mr Angry!

There is an atmosphere of awe, as we make our way to the simulator. I am feeling ridiculously nervous, the events of the past few weeks having done nothing to put me at ease.

Phil nods at me encouragingly. 'We'll just need to get on with this now,' he reassures me. 'It's just another day in the simulator, and before you know it, it will be over and you wonder what the fuss was all about.'

I hang on to that cheerful thought and within minutes we are indeed in the thick of things. Exam or not, I must admit that it is such a relief to not be shouted at – my exam nerves are soon forgotten.

Slowly we make our way through the items to be flown, including single engine work, various approaches and a mixed bag of emergencies.

Four hours later we are done for the day. It is two a.m. as we leave the building, utterly exhausted. We will be back tomorrow night to finish off the 'low visibility' items of the test.

The second night is as stressful as the first. It is not all smooth running but we win in the end. I'm glad that's over! And it looks as if I still have a job!

'This definitely calls for a gin and tonic,' says Phil as we finish signing all the paperwork. 'I believe the hotel bar is open 24/7.'

'I have anything you like I,' I reply, 'as long as it's a double!'

The fact that I have actually passed my 737 type rating is only just sinking in! I am beginning to believe that I am actually going to be an airline pilot.

I get back to the B&B at four a.m. Sleep is impossible, I am far too wound up. I want to tell everyone the good news, especially Dale, who has been so supportive!

Two hours later I give up on the idea of sleep altogether and start packing my stuff. I cannot wait to get out of here and on with the next step of my life!

Until two days ago I hadn't really been sure as to what that step entailed. The roster that we were told to expect had not materialized, and it took several phone calls to Scottish Worldwide in order to figure out what they wanted us to do next. Eventually we were told to make our way to our allocated base, which in my case is Edinburgh.

I am quite pleased about that actually. It's a beautiful city and I can think of worse places to live. So, the plan is to make my way back to Stansted today, and then to Edinburgh tomorrow.

I check out of the B&B and make my way back to Brian's house, where I quickly drop off my stuff. Then I call Dale to give him the good news about my test.

He is delighted. My news puts him in a celebratory mood.

'That's definitely lunch on me today,' he promises, 'and possibly a hair of the dog.'

'I'm not really hung over I don't think, just punch drunk and really really tired.'

A couple of hours later we are in the Fox and Hounds, tucking into our roast dinners.

'So, how was it then?' Dale wants to know.

'It certainly had its moments,' I begin and then proceed to tell him all the details.

'Well, you are on your way now and I drink to that,' says Dale, 'onwards and upwards, so to speak.'

We spend another hour or so catching up on the gossip. Then I must make a move to go and get organized for the trip up North tomorrow.

We part company and I make my way back to Brian's house. Another packing expedition! Now, what am I going to take to Scotland?

To start with, I'm going to need plenty of warm clothes. There may be spring in the air, but I am going way up North after all. The two Scottish chaps on the course have been praising the Scottish weather, and if I was to listen to them, I would be packing shorts and T-shirts. I have a feeling, though, that their account of the weather was based on misplaced loyalty to Scotland rather than fact, and decide to err on the side of caution.

The clothes issue sorted, I think about the rest of my load. Ice skates, now that's an idea! I am more likely to need them rather than shorts and T-shirts. Otherwise ... well anything else that will fit into the car without making it burst at the seams, and certainly all the things I might need until I am able to find somewhere to live and get my furniture.

On Sunday morning I get up early to start my journey to Edinburgh. I want to take my time driving up. It's quite a big journey in every way, and I decide to enjoy it as much as possible.

I make my way up the M11 and am pleased that it is far too early for traffic jams, then up the A14 and finally onto the A1. As I stop for a coffee at Peterborough, I glance at the turn off to Spalding. Was it really only three months ago that I left Fenmere? I had such a good time working there. This job will have a lot to live up to.

I leave Peterborough behind and make my way North past Grantham and Newark. There is still not too much traffic about and I am making good progress. I drive past Doncaster and stop for lunch at Whetherby, just North of Leeds. I was quite fond of Leeds actually, despite the chaotic circumstances at the time.

I continue North past Darlington and Newcastle, straight past the 'Angel of the North'. The traffic slows down a little here, as shoppers are making their way to the Metro Centre, for a spot of retail therapy.

Just North of Newcastle the road gets much narrower and eventually single file. The weather is changing now, and as I am leaving the towns behind the country side looks grey and dismal. I stop for another coffee to break up the monotony of the drive and am surprised at how much colder it has become.

As I continue on my journey the leaden skies have opened and the wind is picking up. An hour or so later I reach Berwick on Trent, the only large conurbation between Edinburgh and Newcastle. A few miles west of Berwick blue and white flags, flying in the now gale force winds, announce the Scottish Border. A sign saying "*Welcome to Scotland*" is almost obscured by the driving rain. I do not stop for long and instead decide to get to Edinburgh as soon as possible. My mood has turned a bit gloomy and I need a few bright city lights to cheer me up.

To dispel the gloomy feeling I remind myself that I should be happy! Despite the obstacles I have succeeded in my venture so far. This is a new start! Things will be great from now on!

The episode with the missing car door (and other mishaps)

My first impression of Edinburgh is not a good one, as the rain is now a deluge and the wind is reaching storm force. The first task is to find a hotel, or even better a B&B, just so I have an initial base from which to go flat hunting.

The tourist information is in the town centre and I have been advised to avoid driving there at all costs. Today is not the weather to park and go by bus, so I decide to drive around the bypass to see what I can find. The traffic has slowed almost to a standstill as the road has been flooded in places. Good job it is only three in the afternoon, so I am in no desperate hurry.

As I reach the airport end of the bypass, I notice a sign advertising the local Travelodge. Well, that will do! I really don't think I want to drive any further.

I pull up in the car park and open the car door. That's when it happens:

There is a big whooshing sound as a gust of wind grabs the door and rips it wide open at first, and then, before I know what is happening, cleanly off the car! My eyes are like dinner plates as I watch my car door making its way along the car park. Thankfully I recover quickly and chase after it, catch up with it, and shove it onto the back seat. OMG!!

As I make my way to reception both receptionists are in hysterics.

'Well, I'd like a room for a couple of nights please to start with,' I say with an expression that suggests chasing after your car door is quite a normal Sunday afternoon activity.

They stare at me. ' … and maybe a garage for my car?' I manage to add, before we all burst into giggles.

'You could park under the roof tonight,' says one of the receptionists as she recovers, pointing towards the 'strictly loading and unloading only' space outside. 'We'll make an exception for you since you have been so entertaining.'

'I'll take it,' I grin, 'plus possibly a room for me?'

I give a brief account of what brings me to Edinburgh and explain that I might be staying for a couple of weeks.

'We'll give you an extra nice room then,' they say enthusiastically, 'in the modern part of the building.'

The room is lovely, although it is on the third floor and I need to open no less then twelve fire doors to get to it. I wouldn't mind normally, but on this occasion I have to make the trip five times as there is no way that I can leave anything in the car under the circumstances.

Almost an hour later I am settled. I survey my temporary home and must admit that it has quality. It's clean, it's warm, it's spacious, and whereas it's not entirely low cost, it's well within my budget for the next fortnight, after which I am bound to have been paid and found something more permanent.

This is not bad at all. In fact, I feel quite at home already now I have unpacked all my stuff. There is a restaurant downstairs and a supermarket within walking distance. Things are looking up. I can relax and have good nights sleep.

On Monday morning I telephone Scottish Worldwide to show willing and to check up on my work schedule. Heather, the company secretary, sounds confused.

'Work schedule?'

I elaborate.

'Oh, I see. Well, at some point you will be doing your circuits, and your emergency training ... no I have no idea when ... we will let you know.'

Ok, stay at the end of the phone for a few days. Well, that's good news. That means I can get my car repaired. I consult the yellow pages and find the nearest garage.

'Ah we can't help you here,' says the mechanic as he takes a look at my car. 'That's a specialist thing. You need to find a Mazda Dealer.'

Oh great, so now it's an arm and a leg job, I think as I find myself back on the bypass.

The Mazda Dealers are on an industrial estate, not a million miles from the hotel. At least I get to find my bearings, doing all this driving around, although it's a bit of a draughty experience without the door.

The experts at Mazda have a chuckle at the missing car door, quote a price and promise to be done by five p.m. That's good news, as it is meant to be raining again by tomorrow.

True to their word, they have the car ready at five. The bill is substantial, but luckily all I have to worry about is my insurance excess and my no claims bonus, but I do wish at this moment that I had gone for a lower excess figure.

Maybe we have had enough disasters now and life can finally resume some sort of regular pattern. It won't be one minute too soon!

By Friday I have heard nothing from Scottish Worldwide. Something is bound to happen next Monday. Maybe I should just have a fun week end and go sight seeing or something. Who knows when I am next likely to have a day off?

On Saturday I get to know my new town. I have a wander through the streets and along the canal and spend the afternoon looking around Edinburgh Castle. The weather is nice and I am quite impressed with everything really. I'm sure I will have no problem settling down here.

Sunday morning dawns bright and sunny and I take the sight seeing bus to look at the bits I have missed. I have lunch by the seafront, and then come back to the town centre to have a look at the shops, although a look is all I can afford!

Fun as all that was I must remember why I'm here. On Monday morning I speak to Heather again, but the work situation is still undetermined. I have a brain wave.

'How about I make myself useful and come and pick up my uniform,' I volunteer, 'or my airport pass maybe?'

I mean I have a car door now. I don't mind driving to the distribution centre in Glasgow… 'Not arrived yet, I see.'

I am a little disappointed. No staff pass means no access to the crew room and therefore no familiarisation opportunity.

I will give it another week. That's another week to …well … study, I suppose. I must try and stay focused. It's been two weeks since my course has finished and I cannot afford to forget anything.

Apart from that I will need to sort out my accommodation. I cannot afford to live in this hotel for much longer. My financial situation is slightly worse than anticipated, due to the incident with the car door, and the accommodation disaster down at Gatwick.

To add to my troubles, I am not being paid by Scottish Worldwide until I have completed my initial training i.e. flown my circuits, and that does not even appear to be on the horizon at the moment. I didn't expect to have to wait that long.

The sooner I find a flat, the cheaper things will be. I have already registered with a rental agency. Maybe it's time I went back into town to see how things are progressing.

On Thursday afternoon I do just that. I catch the by now familiar bus into town and make my way to Clarks Residential. I recognise Amanda who has been dealing with my references.

'Any news?' I ask her, 'keen to find a flat you see. One more week in a hotel and I'll be ready to shoot somebody.' I give her a bright smile to show her I was joking.

Amanda does not smile back. 'There has been a problem with your references,' she says instead.

I'm not surprised. My bank will have finally cottoned on to the fact that my income, vastly reduced over the last few months, has now stopped altogether. I did inform them of course, but that doesn't necessarily mean they would have remembered that when they wrote my reference.

Amanda puts a stop to my train of thought. 'Oh, it's not your bank,' she says, 'it's your employer actually; they are claiming that you do not work for them.'

'Oh that's easily solved,' I say with relief. There has obviously been some sort of admin error. 'Can I borrow your telephone?'

Amanda passes me the phone and I immediately call Heather, who gives me the number for personnel, who put me through to Belinda the supervisor, so I explain the situation.

Unfortunately Belinda is having none of it. 'No, it's not an admin error,' she says, 'you are not being paid until you have finished your initial training; therefore you are not on the payroll. Since you are not on the payroll, you are not officially employed, and since you are not officially employed I cannot give you a reference.'

I don't know what annoys me more. The way this office girl is speaking to me, or the fact that insult is added to injury here.

I bite my tongue as I try to reason with her. 'I came up here to work, Belinda. Therefore I am going to need somewhere to live. It is not my fault that my training has been delayed, and it is not my fault that I'm not being paid. All I need is some sort of confirmation that I am about to work for you, so I can go and rent a flat.' My voice is almost pleading but it does not cut any ice with Belinda.

The bottom line is you are not currently employed and I cannot give you a reference,' she insists.

I am beginning to loose my patience here. 'Look, at the moment I am living in a hotel which is costing me more in a week than a flat is costing in a month. I am not asking you to pay me, I am not asking you to make any promises. All I am after is some common sense approach to take care of a formality, so I can find somewhere to live!'

'I am afraid there is nothing I can do,' is the reply.

Of all the *##! I take a deep breath ready for my next reply, when fortunately for me, Belinda puts the phone down.

Amanda has overheard most of the conversation but does not budge either. 'I'm really sorry, she says, but I'm afraid that without a job reference we are unable to help you. We have to abide by the rules.'

I leave the office in a daze. What on earth am I going to do now?! I am effectively jobless and homeless! Only, I can't claim any benefits as I officially have a job. The situation is ridiculous!

How did I get into this mess?! A year ago I was on a huge salary, with a good job, a house and a life. Now I am in a job that does not pay me, with no prospects of that changing, and with nowhere to live into the bargain.

Emergency action plan required. I drive back to the Travelodge and check out with effect from Sunday. I don't know where I am going to sleep after that, but it won't be here. My money is running out fast, and nothing is going to change in a hurry. I could move in with Brian for a bit, but of course I am not supposed to venture too far from Edinburgh airport, just in case we have to do the circuits at short notice.

I spent the rest of the week driving around Edinburgh in search of a cheap B&B. There seems to be no such thing. They are a major tourist attraction and they know it!

Sunday is getting closer and my search has as yet been unsuccessful. All I have learned so far is that, if a B&B can afford to advertise in the Yellow Pages, I cannot afford to live there!

I decide to drive around the outskirts of the town to see if I might come across somewhere.

On Sunday morning I am lucky, or, let me rephrase that, I find a B&B I can afford. It is tiny, not particularly clean and my room has no window. Smoking isn't just allowed but encouraged, or so it seems. I cannot stand what I am looking at, but at £15 a night I shall have to take it, at least for now. It is somewhere to store my stuff anyway.

I am now in week three, and keener than ever to get on with things. Another phone call to Heather reveals nothing new. No pass, no uniform and no prospect of any training. I am utterly miserable in my B&B and getting quite depressed at the hopelessness of my situation.

Not for the first time I am tempted to chuck it all in, call my old boss at Stansted and ask for my job back. That would give him huge satisfaction, I'd get a few 'I told you so's', and then, when the initial gossip has died down, I can forget the whole sorry thing has ever happened and I can put it down to life's experiences and move on.

Only I am not prepared to do that. I am so close to actually getting somewhere, I simply cannot bring myself to just give up. I wish I could get a job, but since I already have a job that's a bit difficult. I could do with a day to day job where I get paid cash in hand and nobody asks any questions, but where would I find a job like that? Flying instructing would be an option but the airfield in question is miles away, and I am likely to spend more on petrol than I am earning in the bad weather. I drove there anyway to make enquiries but they are after commitment, which I cannot give right now.

I get through another week hoping for the phone to ring – nothing! I don't want to keep ringing Heather as I will probably be a nuisance and I can't afford to fall out with people before I even start.

I spend as little time as possible in the B&B, and spend most of my days in the town centre, without actually doing anything. I can suddenly see why people get depressed and am desperately hanging on to some normality here.

After breakfast, which is surprisingly good and fills me up for hours, I usually walk into town. The walk takes an hour and a half, and takes my mind off my misery, whatever the weather. I then hang around the town centre until I get bored and eventually take the bus home again. I spend the afternoons reading my books and eventually pop to the local Morrison's in search of some sort of food that could pass for dinner. I so miss having a kitchen! The routine keeps me occupied and reasonably sane, whilst I am waiting for the phone to ring. I decide to give it until the end of the month before I call it a day.

The day before my birthday my luck changes at last. After a five week wait, the phone finally rings. It's Heather asking us to pick up our passes and uniforms for base training tomorrow morning. That'll be the circuits at last. My depression instantly lifts as I jump into action.

The episode where things get really bad

It is four a.m. and the four of us are in a taxi, on our way to Teesside airport. It feels really strange wearing this uniform. I look like an airline pilot, but after five weeks of roughing it, I don't actually feel like one. I feel like a fraud to be honest. Let's hope I can turn that around!

It's a three hour drive to Durham, and John, our instructor, uses the time to give us some sort of briefing on the exercise to come. I have been looking forward to this for weeks, but am now feeling slightly apprehensive. As I listen to John, it occurs to me that I have not been near an aeroplane for weeks, and I do not feel as confident as I should. Still, we are all in the same boat, well almost, anyway. I am trying hard to feel optimistic, but this doesn't seem to work today.

By the time we have got to Teesside, gone through security and are finally in the 737 Jet ready to go, the wind has picked up and John decides to take us to Prestwick instead, where the flying will be easier. It seems a long way away but of course it isn't when you are in a 737.

An hour later we are at Prestwick commencing our training. We will have to do a minimum of six circuits each. Phil is the first to fly and has no problems. Neither has the other captain, who has a similar background to Phil's. Those two are going to be a tough act to follow.

'Here come the real students', I think as the other first officer is taking the controls. He needs a few pointers, makes a few mistakes but finally settles into the exercise. He is being complemented on his work, especially as all the while the wind has been picking up making it more and more difficult to fly accurately.

Finally it is my turn. What little optimism I had left has finally deserted me. How am I supposed to fly this thing, I have only encountered ever so briefly, all those weeks ago? I am suddenly convinced that I cannot do as well as the other three, and I have no idea why. I have a go, but my usually strong confidence seems to have disappeared in a flash. Instead of embracing the whole thing like I normally would, I have turned into a little mouse. I am desperately trying not to show it but it does, and John is not happy.

'Some effort will have to be made to keep this thing on the centreline!' His shouting reminds me of the simulator. I freeze on the controls. I am beginning to look as stupid as I feel.

Eventually the weather comes to the rescue. The wind has gone to beyond our limit, and John decides to stop the exercise.

On the way home in the taxi I am feeling dismal. The other three are celebrating their completed base training and I just feel like I want a hole in the ground to swallow me up. Why on earth did I have such a crisis just then? What happened to the positive person full of self-belief, who attacked all exams with vigour and never ever got a bad result? Why is nothing going right for me up here?

The answer would be quite obvious months later, when, having gained some distance, I could see clearly what the problem was. Due to the events of the past few months, and especially weeks, I was simply suffering from acute and chronic stress. But at the time I just thought I had suddenly lost the plot.

Five days later John and I go flying again, and this time I manage to produce a better result, by no means a good result and nothing to be proud of really, but at least I manage to pass the exercise, and as such become an official employee!

The very next day I'm back in the town centre to see Amanda at Clarks Residential. It's time to get out of the den I'm living in and into a flat at last. Things will be looking up soon, I'm sure.

This time there are no problems with the references, and barely a week later I find myself in a flat in the Northern part of town, unfurnished of course until I can get down South to get my stuff, but it's a start. I have borrowed an airbed of one of my colleagues to tide me over.

Meanwhile some sort of roster has finally materialized from Scottish Worldwide, suggesting I am starting flying for real tomorrow, with a trip to Malaga with – wait a minute – that has got to be a coincidence! Surely this can't be...

I stare at the piece of paper in disbelief! Captain ... no way, this chap has got the same surname as Mr Angry back at the simulator.

No, I am not getting wound up! Nobody can be this unlucky! I'm sure it's just someone with the same surname. I make a positive effort to look forward to the day!

On Saturday morning I am on my way to the airport. I am much earlier than the roster suggests, but then I have a lot to learn.

On my way to the crew room I bump into Evan who will be my safety pilot for the first few days, until I'm safe to be let lose on my own. He promises to talk me through the paperwork. It looks more complicated than I thought. Despite us turning up early, there is barely enough time to explain how it is done, never mind why!

I am secretly cursing the disorganised way in which Scottish Worldwide distributed the security passes. I could have learned this stuff weeks ago, if I had been able to visit the crew room! It would have kept me out of trouble.

'I see you are with 'the Volcano' today,' remarks Evan.

My heart sinks! I don't think I want to hear this, really.

'Well, he can be a bit impatient,' continues Evan, 'makes a lot of people nervous'

'Does he?' I feign surprise. This could be him then.

'Yeah, well, he's not been here all that long, actually, only a couple of weeks. But during this short period he has managed to upset quite a few people. Nobody seems to like him. They are all scared of him, to be honest.'

'What did he do before?' I ask holding my breath.

'Don't know, simulator somewhere I think, left there under a cloud, so rumour suggests.'

Oh great, bugger- bugger – bugger!

'See how we get on,' I reply casually, hoping that my voice does not give away that I am quivering inside.

'Well, just don't show him you are intimidated,' advises Evan, 'and don't be rushed by him. Just sit on your hands and think before you do anything.'

Suddenly conversation stops and there, in the doorway, is Mr Angry, or 'the Volcano' as he seems to be known in here. Probably best if I don't address him in this manner. Don't want to give him a reason to blow, ha-ha. For the purpose of this story, let's call him Igor.

He puts down his flight bag and walks over to us. His outwardly friendly manner takes me by surprise. He shakes my hand.

Maybe I got him all wrong. Maybe he has changed his ways now he is flying the line.

'It's a small world, isn't it,' he says, 'how are we getting on with the flight planning?'

Thankfully Evan and I have almost done all the paperwork. We have checked the weather in Edinburgh and Malaga, had a look at any digging in progress at either airport, the weather en route, the likely load, the fuel required and finally our diversion options.

The three of us then sit down with the cabin crew to tell them all the bits they have to know, and shortly after that we are on our way to the aeroplane.

The cabin crew are already on board. I open the cockpit door and enter – I am excited – this is really happening!

'Time is of an essence,' emphasises Igor. He promptly takes his watch off and puts it on the centre console. 'You have exactly twenty-eight minutes until we have to leave the gate.' With that he leaves the cockpit and lets me get on with the flight preparation.

I start checking my overhead panel and putting all the switches in the right position, just like I did in the simulator, whilst Evan is monitoring me. As we are getting on with our task, we cannot help overhearing Igor's conversation with the number one air hostess.

'42 years old and only just starting her career, I tell you. There is no hope really, is there? Let's just humour her whilst we have to. I can assure you she won't be here for long.'

The air hostess giggles.

I freeze. Great – we haven't even got off the ground yet, and Igor has already written me off! Now what do I do!?

I look at Evan, who shrugs. 'Just ignore him, he doesn't mean the half of it.'

I am not happy. This is not what I would call a good start to my first day, and I desperately needed a good start.

Things must get better – and fast. I vow not to put a foot wrong today, but I can't win.

The day goes down hill by the minute. I miss a radio call on the way to the holding point, and make a few more mistakes, nothing major really, but enough to set off Igor.

He asks a lot of questions which, despite extensive studying I find difficult to answer. If I do get something right, he changes the question until I am in the wrong again. The black marks on the scoreboard are accumulating. My confidence, already fragile after the last few weeks, reaches a new low point, which is reflected in my flying. I have trouble landing at Malaga, and spend the entire turnaround being shouted at.

After eight hours of hell, we are back in Edinburgh where I receive a long telling off which is then confirmed in writing.

My report for the day has not got a good word in it, and I am in no position to argue otherwise

I go home and sit on my airbed and try and put things into perspective. Well, it was like the first day at a new school. I am bound to settle into it eventually. With that cheerful thought I curl up and get some sleep.

Sunday is like ground hog day, only worse. Igor starts berating me before I have even left the crew room. He orders Evan to stop helping me, whilst I am trying to get the entire paper work ready on time. It's easier than yesterday, but despite turning up early, I am still a bit too slow.

We are off to Alicante today, and again I am not making a success of the arrival. Things reach boiling point, however, as we are on the ground trying to get ready for the return trip. Out comes Igor's watch.

'You have twenty –six minutes to take-off,' he informs me.

Oh Hell. I have managed to set up all the instruments, but I have yet got to look at the departure and brief the emergency procedure. There is also some paperwork which will need doing and God knows what else.

Meanwhile Igor is reading the paper and eating his sandwiches. 'You have seventeen minutes to take-off.'

Okay, paperwork, now how did this go again? My mind goes blank. I am in such a hurry and I cannot think. I might just get this wrong and then all hell will break loose.

'You have twelve minutes to take-off. I hope you are not going to make us late!'

I summon up all my courage. 'With respect, Igor,' I say, 'It's only my second day. I can either do this quickly or I can get this right; I am not yet able to do both. If you could please help me out here, so we get away on time...'

There is a thud as the newspaper slams down on the console.

'And with respect to you,' shouts Igor, 'I am a training captain, I do not do paperwork; now get on with it, you should be able to do it by now.'

He picks the paper up again with emphasis and disappears behind it.

I am at the point of panic. In the end I decide to do things at my own pace in order to get them right, and although they were indeed correct, we depart ten minutes behind schedule.

The atmosphere in the cockpit on the way home could be cut with a knife! Evan's attempts at light conversation are appreciated but cut no ice with the captain. I am past caring to be honest. I cannot wait to get back to Edinburgh, pick up my bollocking and then go home and die!

I am actually not feeling great, and it has nothing to do with what happened today. I woke up with a sore throat this morning, and I am pretty sure I have a temperature.

Back in the crew room Igor does not even bother to take me into the office. He lets rip in front of everyone. Apparently I am a useless and disinterested individual, who is wasting everyone's time, and who is unable to take criticism into the bargain. I must admit, this last insult manages to catch me by surprise!

'... and you want to go home tonight and think very carefully,' Igor finishes, 'whether you want this job or not.'

'Right,' is all I can say. I take my file and my flight bag and walk out of the crew room. I hang on to my composure quite well, until I am in my car. Then I lose it – completely!

It takes me a good half hour to calm down. Then I start the drive home. My brain is racing! What have I done? I was happy in my previous job. Compared to this I'd be happy stacking shelves in the local supermarket. I want my life back! I want all this to stop – I cannot take anymore!

I do not feel much better as I get home. Sleep is impossible. My sore throat has turned into a chesty cough and I am running a raging temperature. I am reluctant to go sick tomorrow. Everyone will think it's because of today's performance. They will all think I am chickening out. I might be many things, but I am not a coward!

By four in the morning I have to give in though, as I am feeling really ill. There is no way I can go flying tomorrow. I call crewing and tell them the news. Let them think what they like!

The next morning the telephone rings. It's my fleet manager wondering how I am. I tell him about my nasty cold, but do not mention Igor and his tantrums. I feel that the black mark against my name is big enough already.

But it seems that the manager is already in the picture. Apparently one of the other captains overheard the conversation (I would have thought anybody within a ten mile radius who wasn't profoundly deaf overheard that debrief) and was so outraged at the treatment I received that he felt it necessary to report the matter. Well, I am so glad that he did. He might just have saved my life!

The fleet manager is very sympathetic. 'You just stay home and recover,' he says, 'and when you are better, you can come back to work and continue your training with somebody else.'

Finally someone is nice to me! I am *so* relieved that I feel better already. Two days later I am back at work and back in the hot seat.

For the first time since I got here I am actually having fun. I am off to Faro this time. The captain is polite and helpful. My confidence is still very low and my performance not great and it would take me a long time to recover but I am slowly getting better. It's a funny thing confidence. It takes seconds to destroy and ages to rebuild. It is a slow process, but I am beginning to feel better.

Over the next few weeks I fly with different people and everyone seems perfectly pleasant. My reports are looking better and I am beginning to feel like a human being again, rather than the nervous wreck I seemed to have turned into.

I have three days off coming up next week and decide it's time to get my furniture. I am sure that once I have my things around me I will finally feel settled.

The episode with the house move hurdle

That's it. I am organised. My days off have been confirmed. I have booked a flight to Stansted for Wednesday, and I have arranged for a 'man with a van' to meet me at Brian's house on Thursday morning. It took me ages to get a van organised. I do not have enough stuff to warrant a proper house move, yet I need somebody there to help me move what I do have, without damaging it, and without charging a fortune. Add to that the four hundred miles from Stansted to Edinburgh, and there was a challenge!

That obstacle overcome I am hoping to turn my little trip into a social event and am planning to meet Dale for lunch, before packing the rest of my stuff at Brian's. It should all be a good fun.

Two days before I travel the fun part is in question. The met office have forecast one of the biggest storms ever to hit the south of England during Wednesday. At first I am not too worried. During the last few weeks we have had a lot of windy weather up here, quite unseasonably so, and it has never once disrupted our flights.

Today, though, I am not quite so lucky. As I get to Edinburgh airport, I find that my flight to Stansted has been cancelled due to the strong winds down south. The trains have also been disrupted. I go to the airline ticket desk to see what can be done.

'Well, there is a flight to Luton, in about three hours time,' says the ticket agent, 'we can book you on to that if you wish, but as yet there is no guarantee that it will actually depart.'

'Would you believe I am moving house tomorrow morning?' I reply, 'I desperately need to get to Stansted. So I will take the optimistic view and accept the seat, thank you.'

'Good luck,' says the girl as I gratefully accept my new ticket and make my way to the departures hall.

There I call Dale to tell him about my predicament. I leave a message on his voice mail begging him to pick me up from Luton, as there seems to be no other form of transport today. I can hardly believe what's happening here. I can't even get a house move right!

The flight leaves two hours late. If things had gone well, I would have been at Stansted ages ago. As things are I'll be lucky if I get there for dinner, never mind lunch.

The flight is quite smooth to start with. Hah I knew it! A big fuss about nothing!

When we begin our approach into Luton, it is a different matter altogether. I have never ever experienced such a bumpy arrival. The little Airbus is all over the place, as we are trying to make our way towards the airport. Everything that is not tied down is thrown through the cabin. Some of the passengers are screaming and the lady next to me is hanging on to my arm. This day is turning out to be far more dramatic than I bargained for.

Slowly we get lower, and things get even wilder as we make our descent. I look out of my window, seeing the ground one minute and the sky the next. There is another big wobble and then the plane sets down, surprisingly smoothly. We leave the runway and taxi to the gate.

'Well, that was quite sporting as you could tell,' says the captain over the intercom, 'welcome to Luton, where winds are well in excess of sixty miles per hour. Please take care as you are leaving the aircraft.'

I go to the arrivals hall and call Dale again, who promises to be on his way. Three hours later I am still at Luton and there is no sign of Dale. My mobile rings. It's him.

'The roads are crazy,' he says, 'I will be with you as soon as I can, although when that will be I cannot tell you, at least another hour I would have thought.'

That hour turns into two and it isn't until eight p.m. that Dale finally manages to make his way through. The way back to Stansted is no better.

'Trust you to pick this day of all days for your house move,' teases Dale.

'You are not wrong,' I agree, 'just don't seem to have much luck lately.'

We have missed lunch, and dinner is not an option either. Instead we are munching the sandwiches that I managed to pick up at the airport.

At eleven we finally get to Brian's house. Never mind food! What I need is a glass of wine! Brian is only too happy to oblige.

'Didn't think you were going to make it down,' he says pouring the drinks.

I tell him the whole story. At one a.m. we are still up talking and putting the world to rights. Dale has long since gone home and the second bottle has long since been emptied, when I suddenly remember the reason for my visit.

'Better sh..tart pa.. packing' I stutter and make my way upstairs. To be honest I couldn't care less what I am packing. I am far too pissed and far too tired to care.

It would not be until much later that I realised I packed a lot of Brian's stuff by mistake and left a lot of my stuff behind, and that I would have to take a trip down south in order to correct matters.

At six a.m. I wake with a headache, well deserved of course, but a nuisance all the same. At seven the van arrives with Bud the furniture man, and an hour later we are all packed up and make our way up north.

The route is getting to be quite familiar by now. So are the traffic jams. Bud is keen to take as few breaks as possible in order to get on with the job. We get as far as Leeming, when we stop for a comfort break and decide to grab a quick snack.

The motorway services do not offer much choice by way of catering. It's either a burger or a sandwich. Having lived on sandwiches yesterday I decide to go for the burger option and take my place in the inevitable queue.

A few minutes later the door bursts open and a group of hoodies walk in, shoving everybody else out of the way and demanding to be served first.

'Hey that's queue jumping!' I cannot help it – I'm outraged. I have been waiting patiently for ten minutes and I am not having this. In retrospect, I should have just let them get on with it. I would have saved myself a lot of trouble.

What happens next happens very quickly. The youth in front of me turns around and punches me in the face. For a brief second I want to retaliate, then I think better of it. What if he pulls a knife?

I can feel my eye swelling up and my nose bleeding. Then everything goes black.

As I come to, people are standing around me and the general idea seems to be to call an ambulance and the police.

I am not too keen on either, as my priority is still to get on with the wretched house move. Bud had been reluctant to stop in the first place, and I have been holding him up for quite a while.

In the end the restaurant manager gives me a free meal to take away, by means of compensation, and when I finally manage to convince him that I am fine really, he eventually lets me go.

'What the hell has happened to you?' Bud gives me a look of concern.

I tell him the story as we make our way towards Newcastle.

The fast food incident is certainly leaving its mark. I am going to have a shiner tomorrow. This is just getting better and better.

We get to Edinburgh just in time for the rush hour and do not make it to my flat until seven. We quickly unload the furniture and Bud is on his way home.

I shut my front door. This is it. I have moved – now I can finally turn this into a home. Despite the mad twenty hours I have just had, I feel happy for the first time in weeks.

I would like to spend the next day just unpacking and getting settled, but one look at my face tells me otherwise.

My left eye has gone a curious colour of purple-yellow and I feel that it just might be best to get it looked at.

The doctors surgery is only a few hundred yards away and they agree to fit me in that afternoon.

'Been in the wars, have we?' says the doctor cheerfully as he examines my eye. He then decides to send me to hospital for an X-ray, just in case.

It isn't until five in the evening that I am home again, thankfully with all my bones intact. This whole thing has put me off burgers altogether.

I spend my final day off unpacking my things and must admit that I am having a really good time doing it, apart from the bit where I have to make a pile for Brian's things to take back down south.

Now and again I am unpacking stuff that I had forgotten I even owned. It's almost like Christmas! By the evening I am what you could call settled. Just as well, I am going back to work tomorrow.

The episode where it all comes together

My training flights continue and I am making progress at last. I seem to have overcome my initial confidence crisis and am feeling more like my old self again.

This afternoon I am going to see the training department, in order to book my final test. They shuffle a bit of paperwork and finally decide on Tuesday 19th June. I will be going to Malaga.

Malaga is good. I can do that. I have done it many times, but I will look at every aspect of it to be one hundred percent prepared. I spend my week end off looking at paperwork, airport maps and en route diversions. I don't want any surprises on the day!

On Monday I am having a last day of practice going to Alicante. The flight goes well and I am feeling ready for the big day tomorrow.

Therefore it is very disappointing when there is a message on my phone that evening saying that my test on Tuesday has been cancelled for operational reasons, and that I was going to fly on Friday instead, this time to Palma.

Big shame – I was all psyched up. Back to the drawing board it is. I spend Tuesday, Wednesday and Thursday looking at every aspect of Palma. This time there are no cancellations and on Friday morning I am on my way to the airport. So this it!

I get to the crew room about an hour before I have to and dedicate myself to meticulous flight preparation. By the time the captain gets there I am ready, my paperwork a work of art.

'Good morning, I am Chris,' he introduces himself. 'So, you have been through two months of hell and now you are hoping to bring this to an end, are you?' He grins at me.

My God – it's a human being! I am breathing a sigh of relief.

We finish our flight planning and speak to the rest of the crew. Fifteen minutes later we are on our way to the aeroplane, and forty-five minutes after that we are in the air heading for Palma.

I am very nervous. So much pivots on today's outcome! If I get this wrong, I will be out of a job. But now is not the time to think about that.

The flight is going smoothly. I have flown a reasonable departure, remembered all my actions, and now it's just getting on with the routine tasks on the way down there. I ask Chris for the weather at all my chosen diversion airports, and make my broadcast to the passengers. I now have two hours until we get there, that means plenty of thinking time to plan my arrival.

The weather won't be a problem as such. The forecast showed Palma to be sunny, but the wind could favour either runway. There is no point planning my arrival quite meticulously for the westerly runway, if we then land towards the east, or vice versa. The current weather for Palma will not reach us for another hour or so, and I am desperate to do something. I don't want to sit here, look out of the window at the passing country side, and then have a mad rush at the end. I start planning for westerlies and decide to be flexible.

Just as well! As Chris writes down the weather, I can see that we will land towards the east. Still, there is plenty of time to change things. I work methodically through the scan. I set the inbound course for runway 06, and bug our decision altitude on the altimeter. I set the correct frequencies on the navigation radios, and finally reprogram the aeroplane's computer. The arrival speeds will need to be decided for the other runway, and the setting of the auto brake. The latter depends on landing weight, temperature and runway length, and requires consulting a book of graphs. That's it. I'm done. I open my mouth to start the arrival briefing, when Chris tries to catch my attention.

'They've changed runways again,' he says. We are landing on westerlies after all.

Oh sh##t! Now I am in a hurry. I have to change everything back to plan A, and I have about ten minutes to do it in.

Chris gives me a hand this time and takes care of the computer for me. Finally I get to do my arrival briefing – not one minute too soon!

I talk about the arrival route, its levels and speeds, the landing procedure and taxi routes. I mention contingencies in case we need to divert at the last minute and the fuel available to us in case we have to hold. Finally I'm done.

The aeroplane is still descending and making its way towards the airport. In the distance I can see the runway.

'Don't mess up the landing, don't mess up the landing' I think to myself as the runway lights are getting closer. Of course, the more I think about it, the more I tense up. This is turning into a white knuckle ride. I put the aircraft over the runway and aim at the touch down point. I raise the nose, cut the power and wait.

Thud!

Oh great – that's not going to go down very well. Why couldn't I land like I did the last few days?!

I feel gutted as we taxi in, and I do not dare say anything. Just making myself invisible at this point would be a very good idea. If Chris can't see me, he can't fail me.

'Not the smoothest of landings,' he says eventually.

'Nervous as hell but no excuses,' I reply, bracing myself for bad news.

'More than happy with everything else though,' says Chris, 'and you coped really well with all the last minute changes on the way down. So, how about this? You relax and let me fly this thing home, and then you just have a go at the landing back in Edinburgh.'

What can I say? It's a fair deal.

I try and not let my nerves get the better of me during the seemingly endless trip home.

Chris is friendly and making conversation. I can tell he is really on my side here. As we get closer I get the Edinburgh weather. The wind is strong and gusting across the runway.

'That's a bit stronger than you are expected to cope with at this stage,' says Chris looking at the weather report. 'But don't worry, just have a go at it and see how you get on.' He gives me a few tips on how to cope with crosswinds.

It sounds like he might make allowances here. I relax.

The arrival is quite straight forward this time. Before I know it I am on final approach again looking at the runway. It is a bit bumpy but no more so than when I was flying instructing on a windy day. I just go with it and am actually *enjoying* myself. Let's face it; if I fail this, this is probably my last flight. So I might as well make the best of it!

Here comes the runway. I do exactly what Chris has told me to do – and it works beautifully! I produce a good landing, far better than the one in Palma, and one of the best ones I have ever done.

'Fantastic!' Chris is delighted. There can be no doubt in my mind now, can there? Well done, you've passed.'

I am delighted! I have actually passed my training. I am now officially an airline pilot. Take me to the pub!

During the next few weeks I settle into my routine at work. It's so nice just turning up, without worrying about reports and performance.

Once I passed my training I was convinced that I would just settle in at home, too. But unfortunately that has not happened. I still feel like a tourist and can't seem to relax.

I have had to move to a brand new area so many times in my life, whenever my job required it, and I have never had a problem settling anywhere. I am perplexed.

Maybe too many bad things have happened here. Maybe my friends are too far south. I can't really put my finger on it. All I know is that, for the first time in my life, I am finding it difficult to just become part of the furniture.

A couple of months later I still feel the same. I should be house hunting by now, but I have no enthusiasm. The more I think about it, the more I am convinced that I am not meant to be here.

Everything that has happened has been a valuable experience in one way or another, and what I would like to do is to take the experience forward and to leave the black marks behind. I'm not sure where my home is, but my heart is in England.

The lease on my flat will run out in about eight weeks. Why don't I just see what's around and go with it. I have the strong desire to make a new start, somewhere else.

The episode where I'm coming home

Once the idea has manifested itself, I cannot let go of it. I am like a dog with a bone as I start scanning the job adverts. In fact, I cannot remember having had this much enthusiasm for anything in years!

I update my CV, adding my as yet limited airline experience, and send off a few job applications.

Nothing happens for about a fortnight, then I manage to have not just one but three invitations for interviews. I cannot believe my luck! What a difference a little experience makes!

I decide to go with fate this time! Whoever is offering me a job first will be my next employer, well, within reason.

Two weeks later I am on my way to Leeds to attend my first interview. I have no idea what to expect really and prepared myself as well as I could, just using the internet for guidance.

By another stroke of luck dale is working out of Liverpool this week and has offered me free accommodation in his apartment. I'm delighted at the prospect. Cheap accommodation and moral support – what more can a girl ask for!

The next day I make my way over to Leeds-Bradford Airport along the M62.

The atmosphere during the interview is friendly, almost cheerful, and I like the place already. I answer all the questions and ask my own questions in return. Half an hour later I am done.

As I drive back to Dale's I try to speculate on the outcome, but of course that's an entirely pointless exercise.

'If they want you then they'll have you, and if they don't you got two more.' Dale is philosophical about the whole thing.

The next morning I drive back to Edinburgh and decide to put the interview out of my mind and concentrate on the other two, but I never get that far.

Before I even get near my next interview date, I have a phone call from the fleet manager saying 'welcome on board, you are in'.

I am *delighted*! I am moving to Leeds!

Suddenly my life becomes a frenzy of activity yet again, but in a good way. I'm moving back to England!

The very same day I give notice on my flat, and start packing a few boxes. I cannot wait to get out of here!

Later that afternoon I am on the phone to the estate agents in Leeds in order to get the referencing under way!

No silly problems this time. A week later they say I am ready to go and I pick a flat on their website, a modern place, with somewhere to park the car for a change.

The car parking in Edinburgh was a big issue here. Finding a space was sheer luck, and even then the car kept getting damaged. I had to have it repaired twice, each time cursing my high insurance excess.

The new job starts much earlier then anticipated, but eventually an agreement is reached which helps me to escape. That's how it feels, anyway.

All I need to do now is to find a hotel in Leeds for the first fortnight, until I can move into my flat. I wonder if Gwen & Paul's place still exists. I dig around for their business card. It doesn't take too long to find it – good job I am organised!

I ring the number. Gwen answers straight away.

I briefly explain who I am. 'I don't know whether you remember me, but, anyway, I was wondering whether you might have a room on the ...'

'Of course we remember you,' shouts Gwen, seemingly delighted to hear my voice. 'We always have a room for you, you just tell us when you want to stay.'

So I find myself two weeks later, back in the B&B in Leeds, in my little room under the roof. It's like I have never been away. Only this time Paul's leg is not in plaster and

Gwen is feeling much happier. Even the dog is still there, although he is slowing down a bit.

I stay there quite happily, whilst I am getting through my induction week at the airport. Everything is so organised and so friendly. I am quite impressed.

Two weeks after that I move into my flat. It's fantastic! I could not wish for a better home. I have managed to move two car loads of stuff down from Edinburgh. The furniture will have to wait until I have done my initial training and have time to organise a proper house move.

I now have two bedrooms, so buying another bed is justified. That's really all I need for now. Gwen seems to know everyone in the bed store and manages to get me some discount.

Now I have a bed, a bathroom and one chair to sit on in the lounge. I have build in wardrobes and a kitchen with all mod cons. It's better than a hotel, this. I am happy as a pig in clover.

Meanwhile my training reaches its conclusion and I start flying the line. Work is brilliant. I am well looked after and there is no Mr Angry in sight. I am settling in and making friends and I love the area!

My furniture arrives a week later and I feel settled instantly.

At the end of the summer I decide to buy the flat I am renting. It's just the perfect place, and luckily for me it is for sale.

It's just funny how everything that went so wrong for me in Scotland is going so well for me down here. Do I believe in fate? You couldn't blame me if I did!

Lightning Source UK Ltd.
Milton Keynes UK
01 July 2010

156373UK00001B/6/P